Thus with a Kiss

Amie Kealy

Amie Kealy

Copyright © 2024 Amie Kealy

Thus with a Kiss
Published by Amie Kealy
Copyright © 2024 Thus with a Kiss by Amie Kealy.

All rights reserved.

www.wordsbyamie.wordpress.com

The right of Amie Kealy to be identified as the author of this work has been asserted in accordance with Section 77 of the Copyright, Designs and Patents Act1988.

No part of this book may be reproduced in any form or by any electronic or mechanical means, including information storage and retrieval systems, without written permission from the author, except for the use of brief quotations in a book review.
This book is a work of fiction. Names, characters, places and incidents are either produced by the author's imagination or are used fictitiously.

Cover art by Lydia Kealy.

ISBN: 9798339259015

To my twinnie Lyd, who I couldn't have done this without.

To all the souls no longer with us and those searching for the meaning of life in this terrifying world of ours.

Contents

Title Page
Copyright
Dedication
Dedication
Playlist
Prologue
Chapter One 1
Chapter Two 4
Chapter Three 8
Chapter Four 12
Chapter Five 18
Chapter Six 22
Chapter Seven 25
Chapter Eight 31
Chapter Nine 35
Chapter Ten 38
Chapter Eleven 43
Chapter Twelve 48
Chapter Thirteen 51
Chapter Fourteen 55

Chapter Fifteen	59
Chapter Sixteen	61
Chapter Seventeen	63
Chapter Eighteen	66
Chapter Nineteen	71
Chapter Twenty.	76
Chapter Twenty-One	81
Chapter Twenty-Two	85
Chapter Twenty-Three	87
Chapter Twenty-Four	92
Chapter Twenty-Five	97
Chapter Twenty-Six	102
Chapter Twenty-Seven	108
Chapter Twenty-Eight	111
Chapter Twenty-Nine	113
Chapter Thirty	116
Chapter Thirty-One	119
Chapter Thirty-Two	124
Chapter Thirty-Three	131
Chapter Thirty-Four	135
Chapter Thirty-Five	138
Chapter Thirty-Six	141
Chapter Thirty-Seven	145
Chapter Thirty-Eight	148
Chapter Thirty-Nine	152
Chapter Forty	155
Chapter Forty-One	158
Chapter Forty-Two	160

Chapter Forty-Three	164
Chapter Forty-Four	168
Chapter Forty-Five	172
Chapter Forty-Six	176
Chapter Forty-Seven	181
Chapter Forty-Eight	184
Chapter Forty-Nine	189
Chapter Fifty	193
Chapter Fifty-One	197
Chapter Fifty-Two	203
Chapter Fifty-Three	207
Chapter Fifty-Four	211
Chapter Fifty-Five	218
Epilogue	223
Acknowledgements	227
Social Media Links	229

Playlist

Listen to the music that inspired Paige and Lawrence's story. There's one song for each chapter:

Time – Mikky Echo
Say yes to heaven – Lana Del Ray
Last night on earth – Green Day
The night we met – Lord Huron
Lost in yesterday – Tame Impala
Weatherman – Zach Hood
Secret smile – Semisonic
An honest mistake – The Bravery
Lovely – Bilie Eilish
Breathe – Through Fire
Call me a saint – Yonaka
Fall to pieces – Pale waves
Sleeping with the light on – Busted
Little dark age – MGMT
Metal and Dust – London Grammer
Crimson and clover – Tommy James & The Shondels
Ring of fire – Johnny Cash
Knocking on heaven's door – Bob Dylan
Heart Attack – Demi Lovato
Garden - Saint Kid
Wonderful life – Hurts
The emptiness machine – Linkin Park
Mars – YUNGBLUD
I wouldn't mind – He is we
Genie in a bottle – Christina Aguilera

Drive – Incubus
All I need – Within Temptation
Spin you round – Morgan Wallen
Everything's electric – Liam Gallegher
Change – Lana del Rey
Lullaby – Nickelback
Tap out – The Strokes
Transgender – Crystal Castles
How soon is now – The smiths
Linger – The cranberries
Fall to pieces – Avril Lavigne
Snow (hey oh) – Red hot chili peppers
Awake and alive – Skillet
Between the bars – Elliot Smith
My heart hurts – Altas, Lexnour
Heaven – The Kid LAROI
I miss you – Blink 182
Bulletproof – Nate smith ft Avril Lavigne
Hell song – SUM 41 / Vitamin String Quartet
Hurt – Johnny Cash
Last resort reimagined – Falling in reverse
Can't look back – MGK
At the door – The strokes
Seven – Taylor Swift
Twin flame - MGK
Crushcrushcrush – Paramour
The Bridge – D4vd
Miracle of love – Eurythmics
Lost – Linkin Park
You're the one that I want – Grease
My Immortal – Evanescence
Day is gone – Noah Gunderson

Scan to play:

Prologue

The thing about time is that it's always guaranteed but never for a determined period. This is why humans inevitably fail. They fail because they only realise how precious time is when it's slipping between their fingers and they're slipping away. And like everything in this cruel world, time is not given to each person in equal measure. Some bask in the beauty of a century well lived, whilst others fight with their every breath just to make it through another day.

But that is the way of all things. The impossibility of the hand you're dealt is one you have very little say in, and the only way to rebel against the strings of fate is by making those few years or few decades count. It's not enough to just exist, going through the motions of each day in a feeble caricature of living. Instead, it's taking the big risks, it's putting yourself on the edge of a knife to feel alive. That is what it means to live.

The true beauty of the human existence is that it is finite. You can live for centuries on the outside, a pariah looking through the window at human civilisation. But that is not living and it isn't life. Human life is that much more beautiful because it isn't infinite. It will end. Death is what makes life worth living because you're racing against a clock you cannot see and know that at some undefined point in the future, the seconds will wind down until all that is left is one final breath.

And then you're gone.

But without the clock you're all racing against, each adventure, word, action, will simply fail to have meaning because you could go on living those same things over and over again until it all blurs into one. And that is the whole point of living, to win the race against that cosmic clock by experiencing as much as you can, in the time that you are granted.

To be alive means to let go of your fear of the end and embrace it for the blessing it is: that you got to be here in the first place.

Time is not the enemy, you are.

Chapter One

Lawrence

I can't remember when I began reaping; one minute I was nothing, the next minute I was born out of the darkness. My purpose of ferrying those bright lights humans call souls the only thing I knew. Ever since, I've spent my days watching the human world from the outside, waiting for the call of death to wash over the people on my list. Only when a soul is on the cusp of never-being do I get to interact, step in.

They say you never forget your first and I couldn't agree more. At the root of all things, souls are just light, airy substances that pass through the gate of my body into the so-called bliss of the after world. It doesn't really matter who people are in life because in death they are all the same: gone. But I do remember the first soul I took, in the same way one remembers the long-ago story told by their grandparents. It happened so quickly; I wasn't even sure what was happening. My body followed on instinct alone, the maudlin cry of an un-reaped soul, until I appeared on a dreary, grey alley, surrounded by discarded rubbish and unwanted things. I don't recall much, but I do recall the lifeless lump heaped with stained and tattered blankets, my first and perhaps most dismal view of human life. I reached my hand down to the lifeless body, beckoning the soul to me so I could help it on its journey. I wasn't sure what I would feel when their soul passed through my body, but the energetic bubble of life that flooded me left me feeling numb once it had passed through. When the soul had passed on, I was left with this hollowness inside. I hadn't realised the nothingness I was until that brief touch of humanity.

And ever since then, it has been the same feeling, one soul after another after another in an endless mirage. Centuries have passed and I'm living on autopilot, no longer paying much mind to the individual souls I reap, each charge may as well be the same person. I look at my list and the next name appears, or sometimes in extreme circumstances, we're doled out our charges by the head overseer at Reaper HQ. I make my way to Anchor's office to receive my next charge, feeling nothing but emptiness at yet another day doing the same thing on constant repeat.

"There you are Law. Please do take a seat". I say nothing and sit down. And I wait.

"Your next soul is one called Paige Waters. She's young, barely on the cusp of adulthood. And she is yours to reap". Each statement is a fact, giving me very little detail into *who* this Paige Waters really is. But that's fine, it makes the job easier, the detachment.

"She isn't due to die just yet, but since she will die quite young, the Universe thought it prudent for you to watch over her for a little while beforehand. But do not interact. You will watch from afar. Do I make myself clear?", Anchor demands and I nod like I'm supposed to. I've always been good at doing my job, watching from afar. I couldn't imagine why Anchor would think I'd ever be interested in crossing that line.

"No problem sir, leave Paige's soul with me". I stand and start to turn to head out of his office.

"Law", I turn back around at Anchor's voice. "Remember what I've said. Keep your distance". Confused at his lack of faith in me, a small rebellion takes place on the tip of my tongue, urging me to speak back to him, snap at him and tell him to stop being so overbearing. But I know that will lead to nowhere, so I say nothing and head out of his room to start scoping out my new charge.

Paige Waters. There's a cadence to that name, never have two words intrigued me so. And yes, they matter little since they are just a summons of her impending demise. The sound of her name drags me down and I let my reaper senses take over and spirit me away to my next charge. And though her name will soon be just another string of letters in a series of a thousand from over the centuries, I cling to it like it holds an answer I didn't know I was asking.

Paige Waters.

I picture her name in my head and then I'm slipping away and racing towards her.

Paige Waters. Paige Waters. Paige Waters.

Chapter Two

Paige

I wouldn't say I'm naturally a happy person, but I do try. I try my hardest to see the good things in life. But dressing in black and getting ready for a funeral isn't exactly the kind of thing that inspires a sanguine outlook on the day. And like a 1800s Bronte novel, the sky outside is dreary and grey, nature joining in on the morose mood of the day.

I'm not close with many people. I tend to keep people at a distance; life is easier when I'm the only person who can hurt me. Rather than letting people in and trusting them with something as precious of my heart and my time, I keep to myself. And yes, I'm sometimes hit with pangs of loneliness and crippling waves of anguish that my mind conjures for no good reason. But it's a lifestyle I have slowly become accustomed to. The constancy of my solitude is a sad kind of comfort I have made a home out of. But I prefer it this way; my mind doesn't work when there's too much chaos, too much uncertainty.

I let my mind wander over these thoughts as I zip up the side of my black, velvet dress. It seems almost wrong to be dressing for a funeral of someone I barely know, yet my mom told me it would be rude and unbecoming not to at least show my face. As I'm smoothing my hands over the creases in my dress, I hear the doorbell ring. I quickly pin back my hair, leaving two strands at the front to frame my face and race downstairs to grab the door.

"Hey", Ari says, his blond hair and blue eyes a stark contrast to the black blazer and trousers he's managed to wrangle his body into.

"Hey", I nod sombrely. I grab my keys off the side and lock the door behind me.

"Lillith and Willis are in the car but I called shotgun for you", Ari says as we walk down the path, wincing slightly at his choice of words. I smile at him gently, a silent thank you.

"Is everyone from work going?", I ask as we slide into the car, the heater blazing against the chill of the day, a warm cocoon of comfort.

"Yeah", Lillith says from the seat behind me "apparently, he didn't really have any family so Helene told all staff to do their best to come. Can you imagine, dying like that all by yourself?", she says and slumps back into her seat. I don't have it in me to say that dying alone is the peace I've always dreamt of.

"Yeah, it's sad", I say instead. I look out the window and watch as the concrete houses pass by until the grey turns into a blur of green empty fields and grass.

Time passes and then suddenly we're hauling ourselves out of Ari's car. A sea of black clothes beckons us forward and we're soon integrated into the gathering of people here for the funeral. Helene, the general manager of the leisure centre, makes her way over to us, giving each of us a sad smile in turn.

"Thanks for coming today, we're all over here". We follow behind her, little ducks swimming furiously to keep up with their mother's assured leg strokes. I see faces I recognise mingled with those I don't. We stand in a semi-circle facing the priest at the front, Huwet's coffin hovering above the open chasm of the earth beneath him. It's startling to see how small the coffin is. All his years of life come down to four walls of wood panels and the gold details of the handles.

"We are here today to celebrate the life of one Huwet McCarthy", the priest begins and the hushed conversations draw to a close, a pall of silence falling over the crowd. The priest eulogises Huwet's life, from his charity work and extensive coin collection to the fifty years he spent working at the same leisure centre I do now, a stalwart lifeguard if ever there were one. How bleak it seems, to do the same thing day in, day out, for fifty years. I wonder what they will say at my funeral? What paltry words will my life be prescribed to, condensed down into?

Paige Waters. Book lover. Loner. Broken.

At least I'll never actually learn what is said at my funeral and what a relief that will be.

My mind wanders as the priest wraps up his sermon, ending on a poem about how death is a reward for a life well-lived. My eyes travel over the crowd and, though it's rather sombre, no-one cries, instead hanging their heads dejectedly as though waiting for the opportunity to leave.

"Amen", the priest intones and it's like a calling bell back to the real world. There's a loud echoing of footsteps as people make their way back to their cars. I get lost in the languid frenzy of movement and lose sight of Ari and the gang. But I don't mind. I walk back in the general direction of where Ari parked his car and read the headstones as I go. I've always had a morbid fascination with headstones; I love reading all the names from centuries long passed: Theodora, Artemis, Algernon, Ezra. It's like inspiration for baby names in a sardonic kind of way. Although, as the years pass, the thought of having my own children scares me. Why would I want to pass on my inherent failings to those too innocent to battle them? Why would I want to raise a child in this cruel world that surrounds us?

I stumble on from headstone to headstone, taken in by all the whimsical and ancient names. A blur to my right catches my eye and I turn towards it. I'm caught off guard by the most beautiful face I've ever seen. It seems almost sacrilegious for a face so handsome to be in a cemetery, surrounded by the dead. His beauty is unconventional, haunting in a way that radiates deep from his soul. He stares at me intensely, as though I'm the only person here, the mass of mourners behind me seemingly invisible to him. And though it seems crazy, out in the cold and surrounded by the dead, that stare seems to awaken a warmth deep inside of me. His eyes lock onto mine and it's as if something inside me seems to click and unfurl, like clouds finally shifting to reveal the sun. I swallow, trying to rein in this sudden flood of emotion, unable to look away despite myself. His dark hair is haphazardly pushed back from his face, accentuating his sharp jawline. Despite his attempt to push it back, the careless waves fall forward, sitting dramatically on his high cheekbones in a flurry of chaotic control. He seems a sort of enigma; the burnt coffee of his eyes overwhelms me. As I stand looking at him, my hand resting on the cool surface of a headstone, he seems to blur before my eyes. One moment he's devastatingly handsome, sharp angles and depthless eyes, the next he's all hollowed out, cheeks sunken in, his face more skeletal than a corporal breathing body. As I look at him, my eyes can't quite settle on his face - it blurs between human boy and skeleton as though he's a living depiction of a holographic image. Weird. Maybe I have lingered too long in the cemetery, the eerie feeling of being surrounded by death addling my mind. I unconsciously take a step towards him, my body drawn to him by some unseeable connection. The moment my foot moves forward though, he seems to blur, his body and face becoming a shimmery intangible thing, as though he isn't really there at all. I frown in confusion, blinking my eyes to clear my vision. I turn around and spot Ari waving at me from his car and head towards him, but can't help the sudden compulsion to look over my shoulder, some desperate, growing light inside of me urging me to look back once more into those deep, dark eyes. But as I turn around, the boy whose eyes seemed to bore right into my soul has disappeared. As though he was never there to begin with.

Chapter Three

Lawrence

Her name is Paige Waters and she is next to die.

And I know the idea of death isn't nice, but these sacrifices need to be made for the world to stay balanced, in order. It's just the way it is. No emotion. Just cosmic order. Humans have always puzzled me with the way they let their feelings get in the way. I'm convinced that the world would be a much better, less chaotic realm, if everyone just switched off their emotions.

Flick. Switch.

It's all gone and then everyone would just be a whole lot more reasonable. If humans accepted things the way we Reapers do, with grace and knowing to trust in the Universe, then I think life really could be one big happy dream. I always feel this way before another kill, so to speak. If I rationalise and justify the nature of my job, the very nature of Death itself, then it makes taking a life that much easier. I don't relish the thought of *helping* people, not the way some of my co-workers do, jumping into the fray with the thrill of a lion chasing a mouse, I mourn it, wallow in it even, until the only kind thing left to do is take these unsuspecting victims to the golden gates of The Beyond or the fiery realms of The Abyss. That's my job, you see, ushering people into the afterlife, ensuring souls make it to their end destination without a glitch in the system. Some people call us

Angels of Death, others Harbingers of justice. But in fact, we are Reapers. We reap the souls of this life and cast them off into the next. Without us, the world would be total chaos and anarchy, no love and happiness, but unending misery because, though it doesn't always seem that way, Death really does bring peace.

Paige Waters. She is next to die. A young, 20-year-old, with her whole life ahead of her is next on my hit list. Yes, it's sad. Yes, young people shouldn't die. But that is the way the world works, whether we agree with it or not. Whether humans agree with it or not.

My superiors told me to scope her out today and after a conversation with a fellow Reaper and a few nudges here, I'm presented with the perfect location for my inauguration into Paige's life: a funeral. In this setting, not only am I afforded the opportunity to familiarise myself with her, but also, and perhaps more importantly, it allows the idea of Death to sink into Paige as well.

I make my way over to a quiet section of tombstones, watching the proceedings from afar. Though it isn't quite raining yet, it's not far off, and the smell of rain soon to hangs heavy in the air. I can hear the monotonal eulogy of the priest's voice but he's not what I came here to observe. Letting my Reaper senses awaken, my eyes and mind scan the crowd, waiting to feel that rush of certainty, that inherent *knowing* that comes with the first glimpse of a new charge. A sea of black and yet there is a golden glimmer right on the edge of the crowd: Paige.

My heart jolts. I know this is Paige; I feel it all the way through my bones. Like all the other mourners, she's dressed from head to toe in black, yet where on some it is overpowering and forceful, there's a quiet fierceness to Paige that lets her wear such a dark colour without being worn by it. Her hair, which is tied back except for two strands, is the kind of brown that reminds me of sunshine, filtered through with ginger and gold. I can't see her eyes from this distance, but man I bet they're beautiful.

I mean, *she's* beautiful. I can barely see her face from my quiet corner of the cemetery, yet I can feel the truth in it even as I think it. I've never felt this way before, not about any of my victims. I normally regard them with uninterested passivity. But Paige, she mesmerises me. I can already tell that this isn't going to be an easy assignment.

Trying to get a steer on what's raging inside me, I watch the priest say his closing lines and the subsequent flood of people that follow, all wanting to be on their way back to their daily lives. In the mass exodus of people, it isn't hard to separate Paige from her friends, using my Reaper senses to guide her slowly towards me. As she stumbles through the cemetery in search of her friends, she takes her time. Her hand trails from tombstone to tombstone, her eyes concentrating on the names that adorn their surface. Each tombstone brings her closer to me and a tingle of premonition runs through my system. The closer she gets, the more of her I can make out. The soft curves of her face, the uncertain worry of her lips, her eyes such a vibrant blue, the sky would be envious of them. I find myself moving closer before I know what I'm doing, driven by something *more* than just the bond between a Reaper and their charge. My sudden movement startles Paige and she turns towards me. Suddenly, I'm looking into her eyes and it's like the first ray of sunlight on a frosty day, making me realise how cold I was before being graced with the warmth of her attention.

"Paige", her name is called in the distance, and she turns towards the sound, a vague dash of blond hair and a hand calling her over to them. Looking over her shoulder, she nods her acknowledgement. Knowing that she's already slipping away from me, I know I've failed before I've even begun. In the place where Death reigns above all else, I can let my true self emerge. Only in a cemetery where Death pervades every corner, can I allow humans a glimmer of the monster beneath my skin. It's only by surrounding myself in the horror and sorrow curling around each tombstone, that I can horrify them with the truth of who I am. This world really is a mad place to be. But Paige looks at me as if the skeleton beneath my skin is something of intrigue, not fear. And I don't know what to do with that fact. She walks away and yet I do not follow. Though I know I was only here today to see who she was, I can't bring myself to break the intensity of whatever it was that transpired between us. I find myself wanting to introduce myself to her, even though to do so goes against strict orders. So I let myself fade away, using my Reaper invisibility to disappear into the shadows. But even as I fade away into the blur of the Cosmos, I can't help the pit that seems to have formed inside of me, a denial of what I know I've been ordained to do. I haven't even really met her yet and already the idea of her dying by my hand is too much to bear. A weight settles between my shoulders, one I know will probably be with me from this day forward.

Chapter Four

Paige

I wake up feeling groggy, the downcast weather from yesterday persisting in the sound of rain on my bedroom window, a peaceful lullaby, goading me back to sleep. To love the sound of rain is cliché, I know, but the way the rain patters against the panes of glass fills me with the kind of peacefulness even kings would envy. When people talk of rain, they tend to only hear the force of it or the wet misery it bestows on the earth. What people fail to notice is the cadence of it, the delicate pitter patter of each individual drop, how hollow and insignificant one slice of rain is without the cacophony of a storm. Rain is like a musical, full of endless rhythms and melodies, made only beautiful by the abundance of raindrops working together.

Sighing, I pull myself out of bed, already fifteen minutes behind time. I try to conjure up the guilt I know I should feel at being late for my morning biology seminar, but those extra fifteen minutes in bed were just what I needed. I rush around my room throwing on leggings and a baggy sweatshirt. I tend to favour comfortable clothes. I've always thought jeans to be so unbearable, their tendency to rub in the wrong places, making them the antithesis of comfort. I choose comfort over style any day of the week. I grab a cereal bar out of the kitchen cupboard, not having time to eat a real breakfast, and head out to my car. It's really tipping it down now, and like the idiot I am, I failed to wear a coat. I quickly throw open my car door, slipping inside.

My car isn't flashy or brand-new, but I love it all the same. I start the car and signal as I pull out of my drive, savouring the sound of the rain on my windscreen over any music on the radio. The roads blur past me in a haze of grey concrete and rain. I head onto the motorway and groan in discontent. Ahead of me is an ocean of cars, all unmoving, blocking my quick journey to uni. I'm definitely going to be late, but there's nothing I can do about it now, short of rewinding my day, so I just sit and allow the rain to soothe away my irritation. I crawl along the motorway, barely hitting forty mph. Cars in front of me honk and swear, taking their frustration out on those around them. I've never really fallen prey to the whole road rage thing. I mean, of course I get irritated by people who don't drive well enough to justify owning a license, but I don't see the point in putting myself in danger by getting too heated. I take a deep breath and carry on driving, praying I don't miss my entire biology seminar.

***

I pull into the car park, swearing silently to myself. I was stuck in traffic for almost two hours, meaning I've missed three quarters of my seminar. Knowing my seminar finishes in half an hour, it doesn't seem worth attending now. I guess I'll just have to ask someone for notes and email my tutor saying I was ill. It's not the end of the world, but since I actually bothered to get up and come to class, I can't help but feel mildly aggravated by it. The only cure for this kind of mood is coffee. Not that I need any excuse to have coffee. I know it's not the best thing to drink all the time, but there are worse things to be addicted to, by far.

Walking to the coffee shop, I pass by the science building where my nine o'clock seminar is taking place and hope that no one recognises me as I walk past the window. I know they won't though, my presence is as insignificant as a grain of sand on a vast beach. From the outside, there seems to be no real queue in the coffee shop. I've missed the nine o'clock rush, and most classes won't finish until ten now, so I'm well ahead of the next big queue. I open the door and take a deep breath, feeling instantly more refreshed by the mere smell of the bitter coffee beans and sweet syrup that coats the air. There's all of two people in front of me, so I shouldn't be waiting too long. I drink so much coffee that ordering it doesn't faze me anymore. I used to be a nervous wreck when ordering any kind of food, reciting the order in my head ten times over before reaching the till. But now my order just rolls off my tongue, subconsciously coming to me as though it's a second language. The man in front of me orders a plain black coffee. Boring. Though not my preferred drink, I'm drawn in by the pureness of it, how bottomless the black liquid appears. It seems almost infinite. I'm jolted by the colour of it, the familiarity of that dark brown igniting something low in my stomach. It reminds me of something, *someone*, but I can't put my finger on who it could be. I shake my head, ridding myself of my strange delusions. The man in front of me moves out of the way, so I head up to the counter to place my order.

"One caramel latte please," I say, "large" I add, almost as an afterthought. That weird feeling tugs at me still, causing me to almost mess my order up. I frown at myself in confusion. I watch in fascination as the barista pours the milk into the coffee, realisation dawning on me. The dark brown of the coffee reminds me of dark, haunting eyes. The eyes of the boy from the cemetery yesterday. My stomach drops out from beneath me, tunnelling away in a hollowing swirl. I grab my coffee off the side absently, swiping my card on the machine to pay. Why did this boy bother me so much? There was something about him that made my heart twist slightly. How can I ever enjoy coffee again if the mere sight of it produces butterflies in my stomach and an insensible yearning for a brooding boy I don't even know? It's official, I'm crazy. And stupid and utterly pathetic. I need to get over myself.

I head to the library in a vain attempt to get some work done. Perhaps if I keep my mind busy, I won't be so torn up by those haunting eyes. As I walk through the library doors, I'm accosted by a flurry of cold air from the air conditioning, making my baby hair fly all over the place. I turn right, heading for the silent study space, hoping that my favourite booth at the back will be free. Even though it's barely ten o'clock, it's surprising how quickly the library fills up. Walking down the grey carpeted area, I spot a booth right at the back that appears to be free. I slide into the seat, placing my bag on the seat opposite me to mark my territory. I set my books out and take a deep drink of my coffee, overcome with that satisfying first-sip feeling. It's perfect. My day is officially better. Since I missed my seminar this morning, I may as well try and do the reading for it, so that when I eventually ask someone for their notes, I'll be all caught up. This week we're learning about mitosis, which I already thought I knew from school, but apparently there's so much more to it than A Level Biology seemed to suggest. I grab my coffee and put my headphones in. I put on some Tame Impala, a soulful trance that pulses through me and delve into the sea of reading ahead of me.

***

Three laborious hours later and I've managed to get all my reading done for that module and have a growing headache as my reward. I pack my stuff up, determined to get some fresh air, and head outside. Campus is pretty dead, the concrete walkways still slicked with rain, tawny leaves stuck to the ground making the already slippery floor hazardous. Unfortunately, I still have a late lecture before I can call it a day and head home. I'm so clumsy that I take extra care to walk slowly, making sure to avoid any areas that look super slippery. Even though it's late and my mind is frazzled from all the reading, I'm looking forward to this lecture. Since we're adults now, Mr Harri told us to call him Thom, because this isn't school and some of the rigid rules of school life, although not completely vanished, ebb away slightly once we enter the adult education system that is university.

I make it to the lecture theatre and grab a seat a couple of rows back from the board. I take my time getting out my notebook and pens whilst the other students file in. Even though I see some of these people multiple times a day or several days a week, I feel disconnected from them. And it probably is my own fault; I'm too shy to spark up a conversation, not knowing how to drive a conversation past the opening lines of hello. The only time I ever really speak to those around me is when we have to partner up for lab studies or prepare a presentation on a research topic picked out by one of our lecturers. A few of the people I've been paired with in the past walk past my row and I offer a small smile their way. Heidi, the pretty blonde who I worked with on a presentation on the organelles of a plant, waves and sits down next to me. Although I might not know any of these people intimately, since working together, Heidi and I make the effort to sit next to each other in lectures and share notes if we need to.

"Hey, how are you?" she asks as she pulls her laptop from her bag.

"Yeah, good thanks, happy it's almost the end of the day. You?"

"I've had the worst morning, I ended up spilling my coffee down my t-shirt, so I had to walk forty minutes at lunch to go back and change", she laughs, her easy smile belying her annoyance. I laugh along with her, cautious that the lecture will soon start.

"Would you mind lending me your notes from the seminar this morning please? Got stuck in traffic so I didn't make it on time", I sigh.

"Of course, I'll email them over to you", she grins.

"Thank you!" I smile back, turning my attention to the front of the hall where Thom now stands ready to enlighten us on the intricacies of the human heart. As Thom is setting up his PowerPoint slides, the last few students trickle in. We're quite a small group so I've pretty much memorised the faces of all the students in this class, my gaze passing passively over each one as they take their seats. I copy the title on the board into my notepad, ready to start making notes the second Thom dives into this lecture. Immersed in the white lines on the notebook in front of me, something urges my gaze to the front of the room, despite everyone now being seated. A weird sense of anticipation washes over me as I my eyes rest on the glass panes of the open door. Shaking my head at this weird feeling, I'm about to give my attention wholly over to this lecture, when footsteps echo along the corridor outside. My breath catches in my throat at the sight of the boy who strolls through the doors. Because even though I've seen him before, his face being one I'll never forget lightly, I've never seen him in this class or anywhere around uni for that matter. It's the boy from the cemetery, with the dark brown eyes and mysterious face. And he's staring up at me from the doorway, his eyes boring into mine as if he came to this lecture just to find me. Which is absurd because of course he didn't. I avert my eyes quickly, not wanting to stare too long. I peer up through my eyelashes and watch as he takes a seat two rows in front of me, directly in my eyesight. As Thom begins his lecture, I find myself watching this mysterious boy in front of me rather than the lecture slides.

Chapter Five

Lawrence

"So, you observed her yet?", Chief Anchor states, more than asks, making me feel less than adequate. I don't know how to answer. How do I tell him that I was so overtaken by Paige that I couldn't focus on my job? How can I tell him that, after merely seeing her, the thought of doing my job makes me feel sick? I can't.

"No sir", I reply, "the circumstances were less than favourable. I plan on rectifying this by the end of the day, sir". I feel admonished, less than, worthless. If there's anything that comes before Death in this job, it's order and hierarchy. We must know our place. We must submit. It's always been the one thing I hate about being a Reaper - the sheer supremacy of it all.

"Good, you're dismissed", Anchor says, giving me a not-so-subtle nod towards the door. I bow my head in submission, not bothering with words, and head out of his office. You would think that the head office for Reapers is located on some otherworldly plane - we couldn't possibly co-exist on the outskirts of human life. But you'd be wrong to think that. In order to take life, we must also be close to it. Most Reapers live relatively mundane lives, living in seclusion within the dorms at HQ, with no permanent attachments. Those are not allowed. We can exist side by side with humans, but our existences cannot cross over with theirs in any way. It is forbidden. So, in order to co-exist, the head office is simply an office like any other. From the outside, you would think it was a dull accountancy firm, but on the inside, it is anything but.

I head out onto the street, the day dreadfully dreary. I don't bother with a coat, enjoying the way the drizzle soaks into my hair. It's refreshing. I need to think of a way to talk to Paige that seems natural, not forced. I need to get to know her in some way so that I can accomplish my job. But more importantly, I want to know her because I can't think of anything else. There's some intrinsic part of me that needs to be connected to her, in a way separate from the death-bond. And even though I know I shouldn't, that any emotional connection to any human, let alone of one of my charges, is forbidden, I have to know her. My body won't allow anything else. There's a coffeeshop around the corner that I duck into, grabbing a tea and a booth whilst I let myself formulate a plan. I close my eyes, letting my immediate surroundings fade into a white blur as I focus on my connection to Paige. The images come in bits and pieces at first - a flash of the sky, a strip of concrete, a motionless leaf. As I breathe deeper and concentrate harder, a full image comes into focus. Paige is walking on her own, surrounded by tall buildings, the floor in front of her covered in rain. She seems to be walking slowly, afraid of falling I assume. She reaches a stone building and I watch as her footsteps echo down a long corridor, as she passes through glass doors and takes a seat on a wooden bench a few rows back. She must have a lecture to attend. She gets her stuff out, waiting patiently, her eyes scanning each person who walks through the door. What I wouldn't do to be under the scrutiny of her attention. An idea sparks in my head before it's fully taken form, and I jump on it without thinking twice. I let my connection to her take hold, pulling me towards her as I fade out of the coffee shop and into the chaos of oblivion.

***

Before I can get started on the idea in my head, there's something

I need to take care of before I can put my plan into action. With my destination in mind, I let myself bleed away into the Universe towards my intended destination.

Green grass and tall trees surround me as I focus on my Reaper senses and look for Elodie, another Reaper, perhaps the closest thing I have to a friend. I can see her off in the distance sitting on a wooden bench, watching a group of women and their babies huddled on the floor on blankets, drinking tea and chatting animatedly. I wander over, the soft breeze of the day now chillier as the evening draws closer.

"Hey El", I say as I take a seat next to her and her face lights up in surprise at my sudden appearance.

"Law, what are you doing here?", she laughs, turning towards me.

"Just seeing how you're doing and maybe hoping you could help me with something", I grin, hoping if I play my request off nonchalantly then she won't see the desperation seeping through my casual façade. If she doesn't agree to help me, I don't know what I'll do.

"Depends on what it is", Elodie says lightly. Before I can talk myself out of it, I bite the bullet and tell her what I'm thinking. As I speak, Elodie listens to me, a slight crease forming between her eyebrows, but doesn't interrupt me until I've finished talking.

"Okay, let me get this straight", she begins, "you want me to Reap someone who may or may not be on any Reaper's List, so you can take his place in a university seminar that your current charge attends…", she trails off as if daring me to disagree with her. I nod, words lodged in my throat at the sheer idiocy of the notion.

"But why Law?" How can I describe it to Elodie when I can barely describe it to myself?

"Because I want to get to know her", I cringe as Elodie's face clouds with confusion. "She's so young and so full of life, I just want to be able to give her *something* before I have to take *everything*".

"It's not your responsibility to give her anything Law. You take her life, that's it".

"Don't you think I know that El, of course I fucking do". I push to my feet, my anger and anguish burning so greatly inside me that I can't stand to sit still. "I don't know why I feel how I do. I just know that I can't just Reap her soul and that's it. Please El, just give me this one chance to do something other than killing. Maybe then I can go back to feeling nothing", I whisper the last part to myself, but the sad look in Elodie's eyes tells me she heard me all the same.

Elodie sighs and I prepare myself for a final refusal, my stomach sinking.

"Fine Law, I'll do it. But if Anchor finds out and wants an answer to the utter chaos that could unfold, I won't cover for you".

"I wouldn't expect you to El, of course I wouldn't". I try and hide the smile I can feel ghosting my lips. Now I have a way in with Paige that will let me get to know her closely, rather than watching her from afar.

"Give me his name then", Elodie asks as she stands.

"It's Gerad Landlow", I whisper. A crow caws nearby and I startle at the harsh sound. Elodie gives me a knowing look, the crow's cry an omen neither of us can ignore. El gives me one last nod before she walks away. Even though my stomach flutters at the chance she's just given me, I can't help but tremble at the events my reckless decision may have just set forth. I scan the park one last time before honing back in on Paige. As I let my body melt away from the physical world, the crow looks me dead in the eye, and I know that this moment is the beginning of something I might live to regret.

Chapter Six

Lawrence

One second, I'm on the wooden bench, surrounded by green grass and open sky. The next, I'm ambling down that same corridor I saw other students walk down when spying on Paige. But this time, it's my footsteps echoing along the ancient walls, not theirs. The irony isn't lost on me that no matter how long these buildings have stood here for, I've stood on this earth far longer. That these students in their blissful youth are mere specs of dust against the eternity of my existence. And yet, here I am, taking on the life of a simple student as a way into Paige's life.

I stop on the threshold of the glass doors, scanning the isles for Paige. My eyes find her instantly, knowing where to look before I can even blink. As if sensing my presence, she looks up at me, and my stomach drops, the beginnings of something I don't know the name of unfurling within me. She looks away before I can smile, and I take that as my queue to sit down. Seated a couple of rows in front of her, I can only sit and listen to the lecturer, her eyes a warm point of attention on my back.

He introduces himself as Thom and goes on to explain that today's class will be on the human heart. As he speaks, I can't help but be fascinated by all that he says. Even after my millennia of studying these creatures, I don't think I've ever given humans the credit they deserve. It isn't just their minds that are filled with these complex emotions and feelings, but their physical bodies and the various systems that keep them living are almost beyond comprehension. He talks of different valves and the direction of blood flow; the different chambers of the heart and the ailments that it can succumb to. And even though the art of Death is my profession, I didn't quite realise the variety of ways a human heart could die. Though Death, for Reapers, is as ordinary as a passing cloud, it isn't something that will ever take us in its grip. It has always been this ambiguous notion to me, the hows and the whys of Death are always secondary to the thing itself. The peacefulness of the afterlife is denied to those who ferry spirits to it. We exist like time, in waves and trickles, until the Universe is no more than thought in the wind. We will never know peace; we will only ever know this watered-down version of human existence. But still, I can't complain. Who else can say that they will live forever?

"Instead of completing an exam on this particular section of the module, I want you to work with another person in the class and put together a presentation. We will have a bit of fun with this presentation, I think. Each pair will be given a victim and an autopsy of their death. From the results given, you will have to figure out which of the heart conditions we went through today in class is the cause of death and then explain how that condition affects the body to bring about death". Thom begins to gather papers, no doubt the various victims he plans on doling out to the class.

"I have already assigned pairs so find your name on the slide and go and find your partner'" he says, pulling up a slide at the front with various names. Just as he's projecting the slide, I send a quick thought through the Universe and make sure my name appears next to Paige's. People start to shuffle around, nervously making acquaintances with their chosen partners. I hear Paige mumble my name from behind me, no doubt confused and wondering who I am. I turn around in my seat, gazing up at her, the frown between her eyebrows endearing as she tries to find me.

"I'm Lawrence", I say, extending my hands across the small sea of benches. She looks at my hand in confusion and I start to lower it, remembering that handshaking is more a thing of the past. But just as my hand settles onto the back of the desk in front of Paige, she tentatively reaches towards me, taking my hand in hers.

"I'm Paige", she smiles back. And don't I fucking know it.

"Paige", I let her name roll off my tongue, savouring each syllable. "Shall we go and find out who our victim is?".

Chapter Seven

Paige

Like all the other dutiful students, we walk to the front of the class to collect our project outlines. Lawrence walks ahead, grabbing two sheets from the front, and I walk behind slowly, feeling a little dazed. I've never seen him in any of my lectures before, yet here is, my partner no less, for our next class presentation. Baffled doesn't even begin to cover it, yet I'm not one to look a gift horse in the mouth, so I take the offered piece of paper off Lawrence and give it a read.

"I was thinking we could go for a coffee now, if you want?", Lawrence's voice draws my eyes away from the page in front of me. I sign inwardly, the thoughts of my bed and a good book seeming further away by the minute.

"You want to start the project already? It won't be due for at least a month". Lawrence frowns slightly, but the crease on his forehead disappears in a blink.

"I know, I thought coffee would be an ice breaker before we start dissecting our victim over the next few weeks", he grins and my resolve for going home is wearing thin. "Oh come on, it'll be nice, who could possibly say no to coffee?".

"Okay then, why not", I agree, the smile that turns up the corner of his mouth giving me butterflies.

"There's a coffee shop just around the corner if you're interested?"

"Sure", I nod, knowing that this is where it all begins. "Lead the way".

***

I do have a somewhat unhealthy penchant for coffee, so I barely bat an eye at the thought of buying two coffees in one day. But even if I didn't fancy a second coffee, there was no way I could deny Lawrence, not with that inviting smile of his.

I trail behind him, feeling too awkward to walk by his side. It feels almost like being a tourist following a tour guide to the next exciting location. Lawrence wasn't kidding when he said that the coffee shop was just around the corner, we arrive in under five minutes.

Opening the door for me, Lawrence heads inside, finding a table at the back, secluded from prying eyes. The table is a little round thing, standing between a wooden chair and a leather-lined sofa pushed back against the wall. Above the sofa, there's a small painting of wildflowers, hanging slightly off-centre. The perfectionist in me is two seconds away from standing on the sofa and fixing it, but I push my compulsive habits aside and take the chair opposite Lawrence and ignore it. As I sit down, I look over at Lawrence who has the drinks menu in his hand. As if sensing my gaze, he looks up, eyes locking with mine. And I don't know what it is - desire, heartache, longing, or something else entirely - but flamed emotion rushes through my veins as I stare into his eyes. He smiles at me, and I just about manage not to melt to the floor, a flustered mess.

"So, any ideas what you fancy?", Lawrence asks. My immediate reaction, the reaction fuelled by lust and hormones almost replies with 'you', but I manage to quell that response before I make a complete idiot of myself.

"Probably just my normal".

"And that would be?", Lawrence prompts.

"Oh", I stumble, "right you wouldn't know what it is", I laugh.

"My normal is just a caramel latte. That's my favourite".

Standing up Lawrence gives me and nod. "Right, I'll just go and put that order in, along with a black coffee".

I give him a quick smile whilst inwardly cringing at his choice of coffee. Black coffee is like drinking tar, and even if there is something fitting about the way his eyes match the depth of the dark colour. But drinking coffee without milk, sugar, or syrup, is just something I'll never be able to accept. I take the time to look around the rest of the place, surveying the people, the chairs, the staff, and whatever other oddities and intrigues my eyes glance upon. Despite this place being so close to campus, I can't say I've ever noticed it before. I guess I'm more of a chain-coffee drinker - anything with a big name like 'Costa' or 'Café Nero' and my heart just drags me in that direction. This place is kind of nice though, in a small, unassuming way. Lawrence stands at the counter, which is located to the left of the door, the rest of the shop open space, taken up by mismatched wooden chairs and well-loved sofas pressed against the stone walls. I glance back at Lawrence, my gaze automatically drawn to him. I can't explain it but something about him feels familiar or safe. And I know I probably sound crazy or delusional, but I just know in my bones that I was meant to know him. Something deep down tells me that there's a reason behind my meeting him, I guess I just need to wait and see what exactly that reason is.

Since I don't want Lawrence to catch me staring, I quickly turn around as he heads back to our table.

"There you go", he smiles at me.

"Thanks, how much do I owe?", I ask, deciding to go in for the kill rather than tentatively trying to toe around the subject.

"Nothing at all, my treat".

"Oh no Lawrence, you don't have to-"

"Please", Lawrence interrupts, "I want to. Also, you may call me Law if you wish. I know Lawrence can sometimes be a bit of a mouthful". Law, I roll the name over my tongue. There's something about that name though, something about it that rings hollow to my ears.

"Well okay then, Law", I pause. As I say his name, I can't help but think that Lawrence suits him better. "Thank you for the coffee, Lawrence". I grin at him. Taking a sip of my drink, I inwardly sigh at how satisfying it is. I must admit, it's a little stronger than I'm used to, but the generous amount of caramel syrup sets off the bitterness quite well.

"Lawrence?", he asks quizzically, questioning why I corrected myself.

"I think it suits you better", I say simply.

"So Paige, tell me something about yourself", Lawrence says, startling me out of my coffee-induced daydream. What could I tell him other than that I was pretty plain, pretty simple? That my days start and end with my head on a pillow with very little in between. That I have this great yearning inside of me for something more, something profound, but I fear I'll never find it because I'm too anxious or shy to truly allow myself to live, to breathe, to just be.

No.

I can't tell him anything like that, not only because he's a stranger, but because I would never share those thoughts with anyone. They are far too personal. The closest I ever get to sharing those thoughts is in the form of tears hitting my pillow every night before bed.

No. I just need to be normal, to say something normal.

"Umm, you've put me on the spot there I must admit", I laugh, trying to make light of a question he has no idea has so completely thrown me. "I go to the uni just down the road, as you know".

"You don't say", he winks, "so what made you want to study Biology?".

"I like learning about the processes and that you know?". And he nods as though he really does know. "But the thing is most people fall into categories when it comes to learning. Maths or English. I've always thought that Biology kind of fell in the middle. Although it's a lot like English in terms of long wordy things you have to try and get your head around, the basic function of biology is physical. It makes up how we breathe, eat, grow. And that kind of makes it like Maths - or at least to me it does". Lawrence looks at me as though I've completely lost it, and I guess he would be right. I mean, who really cares about how I see Biology in relation to English and Maths? No one. My cheeks start to burn with embarrassment, and I can tell he's noticed because the corners of his lips turn up in a small, not-so-discreet smile.

"Umm, I'm just going to nip to the toilet" I squirm, quickly pushing my seat back and heading down the corridor that says toilets. Once inside the cubicle, I lock the door, pressing my forehead against what I hope is a least a semi-clean surface. My heart feels like it's beating tenfold, my knees feel weak and I feel light-headed and nauseous all at once. Am I having a panic attack? Because I feel like I'm about to die, and that's not normal, not for a healthy young person like me.

What I've never really told anyone is that sometimes I get anxiety - like really bad anxiety where I can't breathe and the walls begin to press in. And the most awful thing about it is the timing; it's unpredictable and sneaks up whenever I least expect it. Like now, when I'm with Lawrence, and just trying to enjoy my life. And it's terrible you know, because there really isn't anything I can do to stop it, not completely, and no matter how well things seem to be going, it always comes back around to remind me that, on a fundamental level, I'm really not okay.

I breathe in, counting to four, then hold my breath for three seconds. Then I let it back out, counting to four, and do the whole thing five more times. Like I said, there's nothing I can do to stop it, but I have found a few ways of making it a bit more manageable.

My hands are still shaking by the time I get it together. I look at myself in the mirror and my face is flushed and my eyes watery, Lawrence is going to know something is up the minute I step back out there. Maybe I should just try and sneak out the back? It's not polite and is not something I would normally do, but sometimes these things have to be done. I grab the door handle, ready to find the back entrance, when I stumble into Lawrence, his face torn up in a frown, worry etching his beautiful features.

This cannot be happening.

Chapter Eight

Lawrence

I told her she could call me Law as a way of getting her used to the idea of me, in the cosmological sense. Although Lawrence is my actual name, Law is more fitting: I carry out the law of the Universe, and thus it is that I am named so. If only Paige could grasp the significance of my name, it would make my job that little bit easier. And yet, she said she preferred calling me Lawrence and I can't help but wonder at that.

I check my watch, noticing that Paige has been gone for almost ten minutes. Is she okay? Do I go check on her, or is that weird? I guess even though I will be the one to take her life, something inside me wants to make sure she's okay for the little time she has left.

Standing up, I head in the general direction of the toilets, somewhat unsure of how to proceed. As I'm about to knock on the toilet door, Paige stumbles out, all but barrelling into me. If I'm being honest, she looks dreadful, but she hides it well. Her eyes have that shiny appearance of unshed tears, her checks flushed in a way that suggests she can't quite catch her breath. It's weird to see her like this, weird to see her go from completely fine, rambling about Biology and her interests, to a shell of herself, nervous and flighty. And that intrinsic bond between us tells me something is wrong, but a kind of wrongness that is almost normal for Paige.

"You okay?", I ask, needing to do anything to make her smile, to make her feel better, to bring her out of whatever it is that has made her eyes looks so sad.

"Yeah, I'm fine, of course", she smiles. And when she looks up at me, I just know that she's lying. Not because we're connected by her death bond, but because of the way she holds herself, tucking herself away from the world, trying to not exist.

"I should probably head off anyway, I've got loads of work to do, but I had a nice time", she nods at me, making her way towards the door.

"Can I get your number? You know for the project and that". She smiles and it seems to move some of the sadness out of her gaze, if only for a moment.

"Umm, sure, here you go". She scribbles it down on some spare paper she has lying around in her bag, her writing small and neat.

"See you around". And with that, she walks out of the door, no doubt towards her car.

***

"Law, are you even listening to me?", Anchor all but shouts, slamming his hand down on the desk, as though his voice alone isn't enough to attract my undivided attention.

"No sir, sorry" I admit, because lying would only cause more of a headache. The thing is, I know I should be listening to whatever it is he's saying, but I just can't get that weird interaction with Paige out of my mind. I just keep seeing her eyes and how sad she was. And even though she did a damn good job of hiding it, I could still see it, it was still there, pushed right down to the bottom as though she could ignore it. But I saw it, and now it's all I can think about.

"I was asking", Anchor pulls me back to the present, "for an update on the Paige Waters case. Your lack of communicating your progress is startlingly out of character. If I didn't know better, I would think you were trying to hide something from me". My stomach sinks at how close he is to the truth. How do I tell him that I want to savour every second I have with her? That by not talking about her as a case is my one way of trying to preserve her life, if only transitory in its attempt.

"If this case is too difficult for you, tell me now and we can get it reassigned, huh, would that be better for you?", Anchor continues.

"No, no, I need this case".

"Need? We do not need, Law. That is a human emotion. Need is foreign to us; all we know is duty and nothing else. And to hear you say such a thing is a worry".

"Sorry Sir, I -'", stumbling, I try and rectify my error, willing to say anything as long as I'm not taken off Paige's assignment. "I misspoke - what I meant was that she needs me; I have already made contact and to involve anyone else at this stage now would just complicate matters. I can handle this sir. Just leave it with me". Standing, I don't give him time to reconsider.

"Very well then, get to it Law - or I will". And with that, he disappears, no doubt going to busybody with some of the other Reapers' not-so-successful cases.

I head out of the office, deciding to check on Paige. Focusing on the death bond between us, I feel myself being pulled to wherever she is.

***

I know something is wrong before I'm even there. I can feel it in the air around me; the way it sticks to my body in a morose cloud of energy is almost suffocating. I decide to observe, rather than interact, watching Paige from the outside to get a better, perhaps somewhat, voyeuristic sense of who she is.

She's sitting on her bedroom floor, between her bed and a wooden chest of draws. Her knees are pulled up to her chest, her head tucked on top of them. And even though I can't see her face, I can tell she's been crying just from her breathing. Instead of unstrained and easy, it's heavy and staccato, pulsing like a beat that can't find its natural rhythm.

I don't know what to do.

It's hard to watch, seeing her like this, and I don't know the cause so how on earth am I supposed to help.

My chest caves in at such a hopeless sight. In this moment she makes the idea of life seem almost futile. And even though the thought of human contact makes me rigid with discomfort, all I want to do right now is wrap her up in my arms and keep her safe.

But I can't, both because I'm not here with her in a physical sense, but also because to do so, to get intimate with any charge, goes against the very foundations of the Reapers' code.

Still needing to do something, I let my aura wrap around her, trying to calm her uneven breaths and give her a small semblance of peace. It works almost instantly, her whole body seems to relax, some of the tension finally leaving her body. She lifts her head, looking around in grateful confusion for the source of her sudden comfort.

But no one's there.

Because I'm not allowed to be.

So having done something to help her, I let myself slip away, back to the office, before I'm tempted to do something I'm not supposed to.

Chapter Nine

Paige

It hurts.

And I can't make it go away.

And when I say it hurts, maybe that's an inaccurate description of how I'm currently feeling. It's more that everything feels too loud, too intense and I'm starting to collapse in on myself. It gets like this sometimes; in my head I mean. I try so hard to ignore it but sometimes I physically can't. And most of the time there's no explanation for the sadness, it just creeps in and ruins whatever good thing I may have going on.

One.

Two.

Three.

Sometimes breathing helps.

Sometimes it doesn't.

***

I'm not sure how long I sit here before the tears finally stop pouring, it could have been hours or centuries. Pain distorts time, it makes it trickle and drag on as if its only pleasure is to wring out as much sadness from you as possible. I try to catch my breath but I'm struggling, and I can feel it happening all over again and how do I stop it?

How do I stop?

As though on the edge of a wind, something settles over me, taking away the stinging from my throat and heaviness from my head. Its's almost peaceful - or at least it would be if I thought it would last forever. But that's the thing about peace, it's transient. You have to grab it whilst it lasts. I look around, certain I'll find someone or something to blame this quiet reprieve on, but the room is empty, just me and my not-so-quiet thoughts.

Deciding to try and stick with this momentary reprieve, I head downstairs to cook myself dinner. Sometimes, it's all too easy to let myself slip into bad habits and just let myself starve. Even if I have to force myself to eat, it's better than the alternative of not eating at all. I pop the kettle on, ready to boil some pasta because, let's be honest, nothing works better than pasta at fixing a good many things. Not wanting to overexert myself, I keep my meal pretty simple: creamy chicken pasta. Whilst the pasta boils away, I take my time methodically cutting the chicken into thin pieces. There's something soothing and peaceful about the precision. Cooking is almost like therapy because it gives me something physical to focus on for a solid forty minutes. Without getting lost in my head, I get lost in the task at hand instead.

Once everything is cut up and cooking away in the pan, I wash things up as I go to save myself time later. It's still relatively early in the evening so once I've eaten, I'll probably sit down and do some reading. Sometimes reading is another way to focus on anything but myself; your mind has to do the work in order to learn the story. And it's that kind of exertion that allows my mind to slowly switch itself off. But if I'm being honest with myself, on days like today, I'll spend all of ten minutes too distracted to really concentrate on whatever booked I've pegged as my next victim, and just go to bed, even though it's way too early to actually drift off to sleep.

But that's a routine of mine, one I find incredibly hard to break. I repeat it over and over again because it brings me an empty sort of comfort.

Fifteen minutes later, with dinner cooked and the dishes washed up and drying, I sit down and eat. And even though today hasn't been the best of days, the fact that I'm trying is enough to bring a small smile to my face. That's all that really counts, the fact that I'm trying.

Chapter Ten

Lawrence

It's late and I'm thinking about Paige again, although again seems somewhat of a lie since she's all I've thought of since leaving her alone in that empty, hollow room of hers.

I get out of my work clothes, putting on a tatty black t-shirt and joggers. As I hang my trousers up, I hear an almost indiscernible crinkle - Paige's phone number! I almost forgot about it, what with my thoughts constantly being dragged back to that beautifully sad face of hers. But here's the Universe working its magic again, pulling the threads of our lives even closer together with the soft crunch of paper in a forgotten pocket of my jeans.

I lie on my bed, hand twitching in a way unfamiliar to me as I type Paige's phone number into the contacts list. Although I have a phone and know how it works, all my previous cases as a Reaper have required distance from my charges. I'm there to take, never to give, meaning that Paige's number is the first and only number now saved in my phone.

I don't know why my stomach dips a little at that thought, but it does.

I'm being utterly ridiculous and irresponsible because of it. But Paige is my charge, and checking that she is okay is just another one of my responsibilities, isn't it? At least that's what I tell myself when I hit send, hurtling my text into the digital stratosphere.

I sit waiting, watching as my message goes from delivered to read without a response. Bubbles appear on the screen to indicate that Paige is typing back. But after five minutes of bubbles and no response, I start to think that maybe she's never going to reply. And that thought stirs a sinking feeling in my gut that I'd rather not examine too closely.

Just when I think all hope is lost, my phone vibrates indicating that I have received a message.

'Hey, I'd almost forgotten that I'd given you my number',

the text message reads. I can't tell if she's being serious or saying it jokingly. I suppose that is the crux with texting, you can never be a hundred percent certain of the intent behind a message.

Before I can overthink it, I text back:

'Surely I'm not that forgettable...'.

And I don't know if it's Paige or the fact that it's late, but I'm suddenly very curious to see where this conversation will go. I'm not embarrassed to admit that I'm kind of hoping for the possibility of staying up late talking to her, the way I've seen some hundreds of humans do over the years.

I wait in pitted anxiety for the delivered sign and the bubble of a possible reply.

'Whoever said you're forgettable, clearly needed to get their eyes checked'.

And I know I'm new to this human-social-interaction game, but I'm pretty sure she's flirting with me. The sick thing is, I want her to be. I want her to want me because, despite all odds, I find myself wanting her.

Fuck.

Maybe Anchor was right, maybe I'm not the person who should be on the case. I'm barely two seconds into this and I've already made a colossal mess of things. It would probably be easier to just terminate my connection and hand it over to one of the other Reapers.

I turn my phone off and toss it aside. I don't want to give up Paige's case, but at the same time, what if I'm not the best person to carry this out? It is pure selfishness to continue, knowing that I only want to be near her because I feel this intrinsic attraction to her, not because I have any interest in the job that brought her into my life.

Frustrated and knowing that Reapers never sleep anyway, I head out into the common room to try and distract my churning thoughts. Before I've even been out of my room for five seconds, Elodie bounds my way, mouth moving at a hundred miles an hour. She's dressed in the mandated black shirt and trousers, her short blonde bob, cut severe to her chin, a stark contrast to the hazel of her eyes. In my time knowing her, Elodie is the antithesis of Death: bright, bubbly, and over-enthusiastic to a fault.

"So Law, it's Wednesday and you know what that means...". Something I admire about Elodie, is that she always tries to remain upbeat, despite the odds being heavily stacked against her. I could count on my hand all the reasons why Elodie's sunny disposition is an interminable horror to the universal laws that govern us:

1. We are Reapers - we take life, we do not part take in it, nor are we allowed to enjoy it.

2. We're unattached entities of the Cosmos. We exist as an extension of Death, never allowed to form attachments, always on the outside, never quite existing.

3. The last case Elodie was assigned was an actual disaster, as in world-wide collateral damage. In this particular instance, there were too many souls for Elodie to reap by herself that seventy-five years later and Elodie is still searching for the few (hundred) that escaped her grasp.

4.   So, like I said, it's all pretty bleak.

But somehow, Elodie manages to stay on top of the despair I find myself drowning in. She gets on with it, with the ease of someone at home in their own skin. And fuck if I don't envy her that simplicity.

"Wednesday means case catch-up day", I smile back. This is basically a chance for me and Elodie to sit down and discuss our latest cases, offering each other sage advice on how best to go about dealing with each individual. Sometimes we travel to the furthest edges of the world, sometimes we sit back lavishly drinking coffee and picking our way through sugary indulgences that humans love so much. And even though they taste like dust on our tongues, there's something satisfying to be said of the ritual.

I'll be honest, this weekly thing with Elodie is an indulgence I should know better than to allow. This indulgence is probably the very thing that has allowed Paige to seep under my skin and crawl into my bones in the few meagre interactions that we've had.

In my own defence, I did try and stop it once. I told Elodie that Reapers shouldn't interact; it was not our way of life. But in the Elodie's typical fashion, she laughed me off and told me someone had to keep my miserable face busy on the odd evenings when we weren't expected to bring death with every step we take. And that was that. Now every Wednesday evening, me and Elodie meet up and discuss our cases and other random human phenomenon that we happen across, and it's been this way for the last few decades. A momentary reprieve in our otherwise chaotic cycle of death. And it's only now that I think about it that Paige too feels like a reprieve, one I know is not going to last long.

"Same place as last week?", Elodie asks, already fading away into the darkness of the Universe.

"Race you there". And just like that I'm floating away too, wondering how much longer I can keep up this death-dance, when my feet have already started to forget the steps, dancing off-beat to a music of their own making.

Chapter Eleven

Lawrence

You would think sitting on top of one of the Egyptian pyramids would become tiresome eventually, what with the endless grains of sand finding their way into one's eyes and mouth, the sun almost blisteringly hot, but it has yet to cease to amaze me. I think it has to do with the permanence of it all. For someone who so regularly encounters death, although 'encounters' seems somewhat facetious given the fact that I am, in essence, Death itself, the idea that anything could stand this long without destruction bewilders me.

"Beat you", I smirk at Elodie as she finally deigns to make an appearance, settling next to me on the thin edge. She rolls her eyes, taking in the landscape that rolls for miles on end in every direction.

I don't say much, not that I'm prone to anyway, but today talking just seems like one big risk. I know the second Elodie asks me about my current charge, I'll spill my guts about Paige, just to feel the transitory relief of imparting my ethical burden onto someone else. But then that temporary relief will slowly fester into shame and Elodie will be too nice, excusing my hesitation away as though it isn't treacherous.

"You first", I nod at Elodie, beating her to the punch, buying myself a few more moments before needing to decide whether to let Elodie in on the sickness that ails my mind.

"Nothing of great interest at the moment", Elodie sighs. In a sick way, Elodie seems to get off on the thrill of learning who will die next. She isn't malevolent though, it's more that she enjoys being part of this bigger story, this bigger purpose, one small string in a larger tapestry. I don't see it that way; how can we celebrate life when all we do is take it?

"I still have all those war heroes and soldiers to collect, a never-ending pain in my backside if I do say so myself. Other than that, I'm currently assigned to geriatrics", she sighs, giving me an almost sad look.

"Isn't that a good thing though, El? You're reaping people at the end of their lives, not taking them on the cusp of living", as I will be with Paige.

"Yeah I guess so, I think I'm just getting tired of it all Law, like when do we get to live? Is it so wrong of me to want something more for myself?", she whispers the last part, no doubt scared of voicing her desires, of getting caught with treason on her mind.

"No, I don't think it's wrong at all to want that El. There's nothing wrong about that at all". I say the last bit again, more for myself than I do for her. I guess knowing that Elodie struggles too fills me with a sense of relief. Although I very much doubt Paige's face hovering behind her eyelids also keeps her up at night.

She looks at me then, and it's like she can see the turmoil I'm feeling, a writhing beast surrounding me, like you would the colour of someone's hair or the material of their clothes.

"What's bothering you Law, you're not one to normally go against our origins, our purpose?". And wasn't that the truest, most devastating thing I'd heard all day. I didn't care before. I've lived on autopilot for millennia, doing as I was told, never really thinking for myself. I've been a robot, following demands obediently, an unfeeling automaton the so-called Universe intended me to be.

But I can't do it anymore. I can't keep pretending that these rules don't chafe, that I don't have a sentience all of my own. That I don't secretly yearn for something more meaningful.

"It's my new charge", I let the admission hang in the air for a few moments, waiting to see Elodie's reaction. She nods in silent encouragement. "Her name is Paige, and she's young, she's barely even begun to live and now I'm just expected to take her life, to take away her chance of achieving every success she puts her mind to. Take away her chance to fall in love, to dream…" I trail off, not knowing how much to tell Elodie, not really wanting to think of all the chances I'll be robbing Paige of by doing my duty. By killing her. But it isn't just the thought of what I'll take from Paige that causes my lips to still. It's the thought of this life she could have had, that I'd always be separated from. The thought of watching her smile, watching her fall in love with some undeserving human steals the breath from my lungs, coiling like a snake in my belly, clouding my mind in something too unknown to me to name.

"Oh Law, you've had young cases before though and I've never seen you this distressed about them". Elodie says.

"I know, but none of them were Paige. With her it's just, it's different El. I can't explain it, but it's just different. She's different".

"God, you sound like you're falling for her", Elodie turns towards me, a joke of a smile on her face, not quite realising how close to home she really is. I give her a weak smile, willing my face as much into neutrality as I can manage. But Elodie doesn't miss a thing.

"Lawrence, no" she grimaces, "you've only known her for what? Shy on a couple days. How can you - how can this be?" she can't even finish her sentence, too overcome with disbelief to find the words.

"I don't know what to tell you. There's just something about her. She's so shy, so unaware of how much potential she has that it's crippling to watch. And she won't even get to realise the scope of her potential because I have to take it away from her. El, how am I ever going to do that? Tell me how it's fair that I have to be the one to do it", I fold in on myself, my head curled into my chest, my shoulders curving into my body, trying to become as small as possible. Trying not to exist at all.

"Because you must", Elodie puts her hand on my shoulder, her way of comforting me. But it doesn't work. "Law if anyone knows this better than humans do, it's us: life isn't fair. Life is made of all these promises, these hopeful chances that may or may not occur. It's full of love and happiness and hope. But this duality is exactly what living means. Can humans truly experience life if they don't also have to experience pain, death, heartbreak? How can you truly appreciate something for what it is, if you don't understand what it is to not have that thing? It's a hard pill to swallow, but life wouldn't be life if it wasn't the contradiction so many of them hate it to be. You can't have joy without sadness, in the same way living cannot exist without its opposite: death. It doesn't make it easy though Law, of course it doesn't. But that's just it: life isn't meant to be easy".

I look at Elodie stunned, taken back by the intensity of her response.

"Has this - have you had to deal with this before?", it was the only reason I could think of as to why she'd given life (something Reapers are generally forbidden from contemplating too much) so much thought.

"It's not about me", shaking her head, Elodie is as elusive as ever, "I just thought I'd give you my two pence".

"And what a two pence it was". I shake my head, tucking away Elodie's advice for later, when I can process all that she's said in the privacy of my own room. Alone.

We both stand, feeling this sudden lull in conversation the perfect moment to depart, both of us somewhat lost in thought.

"Thank you Elodie, that was -"

"Don't, you don't need to say anything", she bows her head at me, a Reaper sign of gratitude, and disappears, leaving me alone on top of the pyramid, more agonised over my duty than ever before.

Chapter Twelve

Paige

I can't sleep, despite lying in bed for the last hour. My mind keeps going back to that text I sent Lawrence and how he still hasn't replied. I think it's just about time that I throw either my phone, or myself, or maybe even both, out of the window, from the sheer embarrassment of it all.

'Whoever said you're forgettable, clearly needed to get their eyes checked', what came over me? Clearly, it was a heat-of-the-moment thing, or I've been possessed; there's simply no other reason I would send that – it's too cringe, too forward, so unlike what I'd normally do. Normally I shy away from most forms of social interaction, from human interest, because it's the only way I can guarantee that no one will hurt me. But not with Lawrence, all I want is to know him. It's intrinsic, this pull I feel towards him, like the Universe wants me to be with him – and how can I fight the Universe?

I can't.

Swinging my legs over the side of the bed, I head to the bathroom to fill up my water bottle. I don't turn the light on, instead, I let instinct and routine guide me safely through my bedroom, into the hallway, and finally into the bathroom with little complication. Even though I'm not ten years old anymore, years of watching Supernatural has forced me away from looking at my reflection in the dead of night, unreasonably scared of who else I might see in the mirror if I look close enough. So, I keep my eyes down and watch as the water spills out of the tap, filling my bottle up until it's close to overflowing. Turning the water off and putting the lid back on my bottle, I head back to bed with little hope of actually being able to sleep.

Just as I'm pulling the covers over myself, my phone vibrates, casting a milky glow in my otherwise dark room. My heart skips a little with the possibility of who it might be. I mean, it's 12:05am. I rarely get text messages from my friends in daylight hours, let alone in the dead of night. I feel sick with anticipation, unsure whether to check to see who it is or to try and get some sleep. But who am I kidding? Until I check that text message, there is absolutely no way that I'm getting any sleep.

> 'Didn't realise you were paying close enough attention to notice, with you running out on me and all'.

The text from Lawrence is both playful and serious at the same time. If only he knew how desperately I wish I could go back to the coffee shop and stop my mind from overthinking, my body from going into a near panic attack. I just find life so overwhelming at times, even if I'm having a good day, that being in my own company is much easier.

> 'I'm sorry about the other day, there's no easy way to explain it. Let me make it up to you at least?'

I add a smiley face to the end of my reply, hoping it will make it seem more sincere, but who really knows? In an age full of computers and gadgets, we're at the mercy of each other's ability to decipher everything through a screen.

> 'You doing much now?'

What could he think I'd be doing other than trying to sleep at half twelve in the morning. Unless...

My phone beeps again with another text from Lawrence.

> 'Not how I meant that to come across... there's a late showing of

Scream in the park. I thought it would be cool to go?'

Oh, at least he wasn't just after what most boys are, unless this is his way into it.

I can't sleep, so I guess I have nothing to lose by going and I can't deny the tiny butterflies that swirl in my stomach when I think of his dark, depthless eyes.

'Sure why not- meet you there in ten minutes?'

I smile at my screen as I hit send. Rolling out of bed, I throw on the nearest clothes I can find and go to the bathroom to give myself a quick once over. My hair is a little messy but whose isn't after tossing and turning unable to sleep?

I pull on shoes and an oversized sweatshirt as I head to the door, double checking I have my keys. As I'm locking up behind me, my phone vibrates in my pocket.

'See you soon Paige'.

My legs tremble slightly as I walk, both anxious and excited to see where the night will take me.

'See you soon'

I type back.

Chapter Thirteen

Lawrence

Yes, meeting Paige to watch a film is certainly not within the remit of my duties, yet I cannot seem to bring myself even close to feeling guilty about it. I wait all of two minutes before deciding to head to the park; it would be impolite of me to get there later than Paige since it was my suggestion in the first place.

I picture the park at night, dark shadows stretched across perfectly cut grass, soft with the dampness of midnight.

I feel my body start to disappear before I even have time to blink.

***

A cold splash jerks my eyes open, my surroundings gradually coming back into focus. In my attempt to appear discreetly without being seen by other humans, who also happen to be in the park at this late hour for the viewing of Scream, my foot caught the edge of the fountain, leaving my right foot soaked all the way through. Luckily not being human has its perks; with one quick thought, my foot is dry again.

Hordes of young people crowd through the gates in varying degrees of scary costumes. Axes dangling from boys' heads, knives stabbed through the unassuming hearts of lonely girls, wolf masks and vampire teeth like supernatural horrors have come alive for one night only.

"You would think that these people have never seen Scream

before", Paige sneaks up behind me, giving words to the thoughts parading round in my mind. I turn around, taken in by her casual clothing and the way she bites her lip. I've come to learn that can either be an attempt at seduction by many teenage girls, or a sign of nerves. Is she nervous to see me? If I could feel emotions in the same capacity as humans, I would say I was somewhat nervous to meet her too. After all, in any normal circumstance, this could be a first date.

"I know. Do they not know that the whole point of the film is to show that danger comes from those closest to you", I take a step towards Paige, smiling at her.

"Exactly, you have to be wary of the boy climbing through your window, pretending to love you", she steps closer.

"Or the boy you see in a cemetery, who's your seminar partner and takes you for coffee, could in fact be out to steal your soul", I wink at her and she laughs. The irony is not lost on me that she thinks I'm joking when I've never been more serious in my life.

"Boys are normally out to steal hearts, not souls", she quips.

"I guess you've never met anybody like me before then", I turn around, sweeping my arm in the direction the rest of the group is moving towards, wishing that Paige never had to meet me, but grateful all the same that I've been able to meet her.

I pick a spot near the back of the crowd, eager to stay away from all the rowdy, half-drunken idiots here for the fun of being anywhere after 10pm on a weeknight.

"Is here okay?" I ask, hoping Paige won't mind not sitting near the front.

"Yeah sure, I brought a blanket to sit on in case the ground is wet", she says as she awkwardly pulls forward a bag that's not a bag exactly, but a folded-up blanket with a strap.

"I hadn't even thought of that. See I knew asking you to come was a good idea". I take the blanket off her hands, laying it carefully on the floor. I kneel on the edge to make sure no creases are running down the middle. Looking up at Paige, from my vantage point on the ground, makes the phrase 'worship the ground she walks on' that much more tangible to me. Nothing has ever looked as good as Paige does standing over me, smiling shyly behind her brown hair. And for just a moment, I'm overcome with the fantasy of pulling her down to me, tucking her hair behind her ear, and tracing her cheekbone with my thumb. I quickly look at the ground, shaking from the sudden intensity of my thoughts.

"I think it's safe for you to sit down now if you want to". Without saying a word, she settles down next to me, keeping a healthy distance so that she's barely even sitting on the blanket. Taking her hand, I gesture for her to scoot up, encouraging her to move that tiny bit closer.

"Before the film starts, I guess I just wanted to say thanks for asking me", she blushes, her cheeks turning the faintest pink, "I normally spend a lot of time inside by myself, so this is cool". An emotion I can't identify flashes across her face, there and gone too quickly for me to fathom it out. She looks down at our hands, mine still slightly touching hers.

"I don't know why I said that, I – "

"I'm glad you did, it's - "

"Look, the film is about to start".

She pulls her hand from mine and faces the screen, leaving me a little confused by her sudden coldness. I know humans are prey to turbulent emotions, but never did I realise just how quickly someone could go from open and honest to cold and distant. It makes being a Reaper that much more appealing – no emotions, no confusion, just duty.

But I can't deny the feeling of dread that's washed over me since Paige removed her hand from mine. Dread fuelled, not by the hurt that she removed her hand from mine, but because I shouldn't have held her hand in the first place.

I look over at Paige, her eyes adamantly watching the screen, and wonder what I'm getting myself into.

Chapter Fourteen

Paige

I know doing this is a good way to push myself out of my comfort zone but being with Lawrence is almost like a completely separate, yet entirely comfortable, zone of itself.

And that scares the life out of me.

That's why I pulled my hand of out his; why I abruptly started watching the film as intently as a lion watches its prey: because I'm scared about how at ease Lawrence makes me feel.

I spend the rest of the night watching Billy wriggle his way into Casey's life. No matter how many times I've watched this film, I still find myself internally screaming at Casey to see the danger in front of her! Most teenage girls don't seem to know the peril of a lopsided smile and dark eyes, but it's safe to say that I do, years of watching this film has taught me that, if nothing else.

When the film ends, Lawrence looks over at me and smiles, a small dimple appearing on his left cheek. He asks me if I enjoyed the film, I nod, grabbing his offered hand to help me stand. I try to think of something to say, but I stand there like a loser, frazzled by too much social anxiety and awkwardness to smoothly move this exchange in a positive direction.

"Here, I'll do that", Lawrence insists as he bends down to navigate folding up the blanket. I start to laugh, watching him try and figure out how to fold correctly is like watching your neighbours argue on the street, embarrassing but also mildly addictive.

"Need a hand with that?", I take the blanket off him and wrap it up in under three moves.

"Impressive, who knew folding up a blanket could be so easy", he laughs with me. He takes the now-folded blanket back off me and swings it over his arm, tilting his head to indicate we should start walking.

"Have you had fun?".

"Yeah it's been good, there's something different about watching that film outside in the dark, it adds another layer to it", I reply.

"You're right actually, it does, doesn't it". Lawrence nods thoughtfully as we meander our way through the mass of teenagers and shrubbery. When we get to the entrance of the park, Lawrence stops, no doubt ready to bid this night farewell.

"I can walk you home if you like? You shouldn't be out at this time on your own", he offers.

"Oh, yeah okay then, thank you", I blush. I'd already mentally said my goodbyes, so I'm thrown a little by this gesture. "It's not a far walk at all, maybe ten minutes".

"Ten minutes or ten hours wouldn't matter me to me", Lawrence winks, grabbing my hand and pulling me along.

"It's this way", laughing, correcting the direction Lawrence was heading.

We walk in companionable silence. I'm never normally out at this time, so it's nice to just take in the silence. It's quiet outside. The kind of quiet that chills your soul. I stare at the sky, my mind finally lulled by the vastness of it all.

"You okay there, you look like you're a million miles away?". And I guess in some sense I am. I tell Lawrence this.

"What do you mean?".

"Do you ever wonder why we're all here, like what is the point of it all? And I know no one can really ever answer this question, but sometimes life just feels so overwhelming. Take the sky for example, look at all the stars. We see their light only after they've been dead for a thousand years. And I don't find that intriguing, I find it sad, tragic. Stars only get recognition once they're gone: their beauty only reaches us long after they fail to exist. I don't want that. I want to, I *need* to, be seen when I'm still here so I know that I mattered". I stop talking, realising one simple question turned into a philosophical meltdown on my part.

I peer over at Lawrence through my hair, slightly horrified by the tangent I just went off on. I don't know what it is about him, but he makes me want to open up my insides for him to explore. Talking to him comes as easy to me as breathing.

Lawrence opens his mouth as if to respond, but seemingly closes it again. He looks like a fish out of water, struggling to breathe.

I look away, knowing I've probably overdone it.

We walk in silence until we reach my flat.

"Well, this is me", I nod towards the front door. He still doesn't say anything, he's just looking at me as if we don't even speak the same language. I wait for him to say something, to do something, but he doesn't.

"Erm, I can take my blanket back now, thank you. And thanks again for tonight, it was fun". I awkwardly lean over to grab my blanket back, my arms brushing his side as I do so. The silence is palpable, writhing with all the words I said and all the words he didn't. He releases my blanket, stepping forward to place it on my shoulder. As he moves back, his thumb brushes my cheekbone, as if wiping away a tear. His hand lingers for the briefest of moments and despite his lack of words, his touch somehow conveys so much more. Means so much more.

A dog next door barks, which startles Lawrence into action. He steps back and gives me a smile.

"I've had fun too, see you around Paige". After one final nod, he heads back down the street and I head into my apartment.

I throw the blanket-bag over my kitchen chair and head back into my bedroom for a few hours of sleep. Once settled, I fall asleep to dreams of dark eyes and lopsided smiles

Chapter Fifteen

Lawrence

I don't want that. I want to, I need to, be seen when I'm still here so I know that I mattered.

Paige's words rattle in my head all the way back to Reaper HQ. And I can't help but feel like I failed her in some way. She started opening up to me and what did I do? I just walked by her side, unable to articulate a response because how could I put into words that I, a chain in the ever-growing Universe whose fundamental purpose is to question nothing and to exist without autonomy, have been questioning everything since the first time I saw her face.

Shaking my head, I let the night wash over me, let Paige's words wash over me for what must be the fifth time in the last ten minutes. The human world looks different at night, more relaxed. There's so much potential in the darkness because, without sight, anything can exist or grow. It's in this darkness that I let images of Paige run through my mind: her shy smile, the way she twists her rings around her fingers when she's nervous, the sadness that she sometimes can't quite hide in her eyes. Sadness that has no place in the eyes of such a young person, someone who has so much left to see. But that's the thing about humans, or at least it's something that I am starting to learn, sadness doesn't need a reason to exist; it exists because the Universe demands balance. In order to live with happiness, it must have a counterpart. But much of humanity is troubled with sadness that goes deeper than one hard day; in some people it runs so deep that they drown in it, slowly being consumed by their darkest thoughts to the point where they become them. I see a little of that sadness in Paige's eyes. I'm determined to at least try and alleviate some of it before I have to end her life.

***

I reach HQ in under twenty minutes, jumping between walking and Reaper-walking to get there in half the time. The door is locked when I arrive, so I resort to levitating through my bedroom window to avoid any terse words from Anchor. If he thinks I'm sneaking off to see Paige or not focused solely on my mission, he'll assign her to someone else. And I cannot let that happen.

Trying not to think of Paige and all the things I don't want to identify too closely, I get changed and slip into bed. Knowing I won't sleep, because Reapers don't need sleep the same way humans do, I hope my body can rest all the same.

Chapter Sixteen

Lawrence

Sirens.
Shouts.
Mayhem.

I startle to sounds of chaos as flashing lights drive past our building, distress alarms being activated on every floor of our office. With little thought, I'm up and out of bed, dressed and opening my door to see what's happening.

Elodie is already making her way down to my room, handing me what is comparable to a walkie-talkie device to the human understanding. In reality, it is much more complex, doing far more than allowing us to communicate over long periods.

"Do you know what's going on?", I ask, taking the not-walkie-talkie device from Elodie and strapping it to my belt.

"There's been a fire across town in one of the apartment buildings, all hands-on deck in making sure all souls make it to their correct locations".

Immediately my thoughts turn to Paige who lives in an apartment building. But as my charge, I know it isn't her time yet.

"Let's pair up, you lead the way", I nod to Elodie, floating away into the abyss behind her.

***

I've seen a fair share of fires in my time, but something about this fire feels eerie, out of place in an otherwise quiet neighbourhood. Smoke pours out the top half of the building, billowing in the wind, refusing to be doused by the water the fire trucks spew out. Blackened brick and debris are all that seem to remain of the lower portion, making the top perilous to any who would venture inside to rescue any remaining victims. Although, by the vast amount of Cosmic energy depicted by my walkie-talkie, and the ever-growing circle of spirits in my field of vision, I would venture a guess that there are little to no survivors of this calamity.

If I were human, I would feel an overwhelming sense of devastation.

Instead, I feel empty.

Devoid of anything.

A black void waiting to be filled with the souls I'm about to reap.

At least that's what I tell myself as I make my way over to reap my first soul of the day.

Chapter Seventeen

Lawrence

If I were an addict, and the ecstasy of drugs actually worked on my Reaper body, I would imagine that this is what being high feels like for mortals.

Infinite and intoxicating.

Numbing disorientation.

It is everything and nothing all at once.

And a sick part of me could never not-reap, if only to not lose the euphoria that reaping a soul grants me. Because it fills me with the human emotions I so tragically lack.

My boots crunch over burnt pieces of wood and crumbling bricks; I'm barely aware of the scorched earth beneath my feet as my hands automatically reach out towards victim number one, towards my perverted salvation.

Touching a soul is nothing like touching a human body - there's no contact in the physical sense; it's like caressing someone's most intimate thoughts, secrets, hopes, dreams. And watching them die. Most victims aren't even aware of it happening – one moment they're in the physical world, experiencing life, the next they're surrounded by whatever their personal afterlife looks like.

My first victim is an old woman, blinking in the dusky air with confusion. If I had to ask for a victim, she would be the perfect one because I'm not taking anything from her that isn't expected. When you get to her age, when you've lived a good eighty years, dying isn't a matter of if, it's just a question of when. Perhaps it would have been gentler for her to pass away in her sleep, but the Universe couldn't have given her a better life, that is to say a long one.

As I take her hand, marred with soot and lined with age, her body sighs almost involuntarily. Nothing happens at first, but I hold on until her soul is ready to depart. As her soul lets go, I'm filled with infinity, drifting so far into this bliss that it's almost a struggle to pull myself back from. I close my eyes, picturing the afterlife, though I am not permitted into it, I can ferry souls right to the edge where they can continue their existence in uninterrupted bliss. As my eyes open, and I take in my surroundings, I'm reminded again how conscious the Universe truly is. It isn't a construct, isn't a series of planets and dust, isn't the romantic idea born of mortal fear of the unknown. It is a breathing ecosystem of everything. I pass forgotten planets and lone stars, making my way to The Beyond. In both hours and no time at all, I'm hovering on the edge of an endless stretch of darkness, illuminated by small lights moving in waves across the black canvas – souls.

This is where I leave her. I let go of her incorporeal hand, a small smile playing along the edges of her blurred outline. And then just like that, she becomes yet another small light bobbing across that distant darkness, nothing more than a wisp of light making its journey to the end of the world.

The second her soul departs, my body is transported back to earth, not permitted, even for a single moment, to linger so close to that mysterious 'After'. Things seemed to have calmed down by a small measure. The human firefighters appear to have stabilised the building, now focusing on recording any absences from the masses and getting the injured to the hospital. I join my fellow Reapers in looking after the remaining souls, transporting one after another until all but one remains. A young boy, no older than ten.

"I'll take this one", Elodie says to the group of us, something like regret filling her eyes. And maybe it's that quiet pain in her eyes and resignation towards what is inevitable, but I step forward before she has a chance, reaching my arms out to take this little soul ahead of his time.

It takes his soul a while before it relents and comes with me, confusion and fear wrapped so tightly around his essence, that the high of a soul's energy turns to ice in my veins. I hear his small voice in my head, crying to go back to his family. It's an effort of sheer will to move between the realms, travelling past stars and galaxies, back again to the edge of that darkness. And even though I know this is the Universe's will, fuck if it doesn't make me feel like a villain. Because, despite the knowledge that not reaping this poor boy's soul would cause a mayhem of cosmic build up, it doesn't seem right that he should be denied that chance of growing up, simply because the will of some omniscient energy determines it.

I let his hand go, his small light eddying across the darkness. I can feel that insistent tug, forcing me back to earth, but I fight against it. I will not leave him, not yet. I can't change the course of the Universe, but I can make sure his little soul doesn't have to pass on alone, scared and unsure. A small act of defiance maybe, but one I would do a hundred times over if only to dull that crippling voice in my head that says I can't do this anymore. A voice that sounds an awful lot like Paige's. I watch as his soul makes its way so far into the black that his light is no longer visible. Only now do I allow myself to warp and shift, becoming nothing as I float back down to earth. For the first time in my long existence, I wonder if maybe being nothing would be a blessing.

Chapter Eighteen

Paige

Lawrence texted this morning asking about starting the project. I had lectures until three, so I told him to meet me in the library at half past because we'll have access to more books we might need for the presentation by working in the library. Since I normally go to the quiet zone when studying, I look around in search of somewhere comfy yet spacious to set up whilst I wait for Lawrence to arrive. With it being later in the afternoon, the library is starting to quieten down, so I'm able to grab a fairly big table with four chairs at the back of one of the literature stacks. I send Lawrence a pin of my location, so he doesn't get lost in the labyrinth of isles in search of me. He replies saying he'll be five minutes, so I start unpacking: first my laptop, then my notebook, then my pens and some A3 paper to use for brainstorming. My array of felt tips and highlighters is a pride of mine and I line up each pen next to another to create a veritable rainbow on the table. I'm just logging onto my laptop as I hear footsteps from behind me; I turn in time to see Lawrence saunter up the stairs, two drinks in his hands and a lazy smile on his face as he tips his head toward me in greeting.

"I got us these to keep us motivated through our project", he says handing me over a coffee cup. I take a sip and let the warm liquid wash down my throat, pleasure filling my veins at both the syrupy and bitter taste, but also the thoughtful gesture.

"Thank you, and you remembered what I like", I smile at him. Lawrence takes his seat and taps his hands on the table, as though unsure of what to do now.

"I had a look at the project and I don't think it will take too long. It seems our victim has a pretty straightforward death, if such a thing exists. I was thinking we could start by explaining how the victim died and then go into the details of what kind of things caused such a death".

Lawrence is nodding along, his eyes skimming the page in front of him.

"I agree, sounds good to me. So, what do you think caused our victim's death? I have my ideas, but I'd like to hear yours first", he winks at me, a subtle blink of his eyelid, and I have to look back at the table to keep from blushing too much.

"Based on the fact that he had high cholesterol levels in his blood and one of his main arteries leading to his heart was blocked, I would say he had a heart attack. The high cholesterol in his blood could have led to plaques forming, which if ruptured, can cause blood clots that block the blood flow to the heart. Wouldn't you agree?", I ask, although I'm fairly certain he can't disagree; this is a classic case of a heart attack. Lawrence's eyes look a little glazed over as if he's lost somewhere in my words.

"Are you okay?", I ask him, still waiting for his response.

"Yeah sorry, I'm just a little behind on the reading, but I agree". Behind on the reading? This is basic biology you normally learn at school; this module is more a recap of things we've already been taught than learning anything brand new.

"That's okay", I reply. I grab a piece of paper, writing 'heart attack' in the centre and draw a bubble around it. "I thought we could make it a case study, give our victim a life before his death. Give him a personality and hobbies, that kind of thing. We can also give him negative behaviours or lifestyle choices that would have contributed to his untimely demise".

"Yeah, I like that idea, it seems only right to give him a life before killing him". There's something sorrowful in Lawrence's eyes, as if this conversation is too close for comfort, striking some unseen nerve. I nod along, not entirely sure what to say. We spend the next couple of hours switching between mapping out our victim's life and getting to know each other. I tell Lawrence about my family and the friends I have from lifeguarding, and he sits and nods along like my life is something fascinating. When in reality, it's anything but. I talk to him about the fraught relationship I have with my parents and how moving away for uni has made it even more strained. I love my family, of course I do, but when all my parents do is judge my chosen solitude, so different from their outgoing, unapologetic social lives, it's hard not to feel like a total let down when I'm with them.

"You shouldn't feel less than for not wanting to live your life the same way as them", Lawrence speaks into his empty coffee cup instead of meeting my eyes, but I can hear the fire behind his words, the conviction. I shrug my shoulders and when I don't respond, Lawrence lifts his head and meets my gaze.

"You should never, not for one minute, apologise for who you are Paige. Never". And still, that fire is in his words now sparking across the table, a direct tightrope connecting his eyes to mine. I open my mouth to say something, but the words fail me.

"Lawrence", I begin, "thank you", I breathe. He nods and gives me one of his lopsided smiles and I find myself smiling with him. He nips to the toilet and while he's gone, I send my mom a quick text asking if she's around at the weekend so I can visit. She texts me back immediately saying yes and I reply to plan out the details.

Once Lawrence returns, we get down to giving our victim a life. We decide to call our victim Toby, a fifty-five-year-old male with a receding hairline and two children he adores. He got a job straight after school as a construction worker, spending the weekends drinking too much alcohol with his friends and falling in love with the girl next door. They got married and he got an office job to pay for the big house they wanted and the two kids they would eventually have. The tedium of his nine-t0-five led to unhealthy habits of fast food for lunch and a rather sedentary lifestyle. His wife no longer saw the strapping boy she fell in love with, but a weary old man whose belly wobbled too much in laughter and whose face turned red instantly at the slightest annoyance.

"It's almost bleak, isn't it? The way his life seems to have unravelled before him". Lawrence startles me, his voice echoing in the relative quiet of the library.

"Yeah, I guess it is". I finish writing out Toby's story and we decide to call it a day for now. Lawrence helps me pack everything up, getting up from the table and putting the coffee cups in the nearest bin. Lawrence picks up my bag for me, slinging it across his shoulder and gestures with his hand that he'll follow me out.

"Got much planned for the evening?", Lawrence pulls me to a stop outside the large metal doors of the library, the slight drizzle of rain causing his hair to curl at the ends. What I want to say is get out of the rain, but I can't quite bring myself to.

"I think I might read. I started a new book yesterday. It was a struggle to put it down it was so good".

"That sounds nice. Can I walk you home?".

I shake my head. "I actually drove", he seems to deflate a little, as though let down by the thought of not being able to carry out his gentlemanly duties. "But you can walk to me to my car if you want? The car park is about ten minutes from here".

"Sure", he smiles with such earnestness the rain seems not to touch it.

"Do you have much planned tonight?", I ask, taking in the light haze of rain that settles over campus as we make our way to my car.

"Nothing of interest", he says vaguely and looks to the floor. We pass the next five minutes in silence, the rain dampening my hair and clothes, Lawrence a quiet yet steady presence at my side.

"Well, this is me", I point to my car.

"Have a good evening, I'll text you soon to arrange something". He hands my bag back over to me and I open my car door, ready to get in.

"Do you need a lift anywhere?", I ask, not quite ready for our time together to end.

"No, I'm okay thank you", and Lawrence walks away, the rain now falling heavier, obscuring his silhouette from view. I turn the engine on and buckle up, ready to drive home and finally get out of the rain.

Chapter Nineteen

Paige

Yesterday working on the project with Lawrence was nice. Even though we were just hanging out together because of the project, I enjoyed spending time with someone other than work friends or my fictional boyfriends who I spend most evenings fawning over. Allowing myself the indulgence of a lie in, it's already half ten before I force my legs over the side of the bed and head into my bathroom. Splashing my face with cold water, I cringe at the icy sting against my cheeks. Once I've washed my face, I go about my morning routine of applying moisturiser and brushing my teeth for their allotted two minutes.

I said I'd visit my parents today which I'm already regretting. I love my family in the way you're forced to because you share blood, but my mom's opinionated personality and dad's condescension are one of the reasons I decided to go to uni so far away – to escape feeling like a constant disappointment. But we do what we must and so I get ready, putting in a little more effort into my appearance in the hopes my mom will find little fault in it. Dressed in a thick cream jumper dress, boots and tights, I make myself a coffee for the journey, lock up and head out the door. I select a playlist of my favourite songs and gear up for the two-and-a-half-hour drive ahead of me.

***

It didn't take me two and a half hours to get here. It took me four.

The traffic on the motorway was so bad that half of the journey was spent in stand-still traffic. In a bad mood from the drive, I plaster a smile on my face as I make my way past the sprawling green grass out front and to the front door of my parents' house. Like mine, their door is painted red, and it's the only thing about this house that fills me with a warm fondness. I knock three times and wait patiently for the door to open.

"You're late", my dad says as he opens the door, the bicycle moustache he insists is still in fashion turning down at the corners.

"I know, sorry, traffic was terrible", I kiss him on the cheek as he ushers me inside.

"Your mother is in the living room", he says by way of farewell, heading down the corridor to his office to work, despite it being the weekend. I walk the short distance to the living room, my shoes squeaking on the smooth wooden floor. My mom is sitting on the sofa reading the newspaper, a cup of tea on the small table to her right.

"Hi mom", I say, "sorry for being late, the traffic was worse than I thought".

"No worries, it happens", she responds, only looking up at me once she's finished reading the page of her paper. "Your hair is looking long", she notes whilst giving me a once over, "perhaps it's time you got a haircut". I stifle the urge to roll my eyes.

"Perhaps", I say apathetically and sit across from her on one of the velvet armchairs.

"So, tell me what's new with you", she finally puts the newspaper down, placing her hands delicately in her lap.

"Not a lot. Just been focusing on getting my uni work done and picking shifts up at the leisure centre". And getting flustered over a boy with dark brown hair, a jaw to die for and unfathomably depthless eyes, I don't say.

"And your grades, what are they like?"

"I've been getting 2:1s or firsts on most assignments which is good", I smile, proud at myself for how hard I've worked to get those grades.

"Well, well done. Me and your father are extremely proud", she smiles at me and for once there's some warmth behind what is otherwise a bland, cookie-cutter expression.

"Thanks mom", I nod at her, public displays of affection not something normally expressed in our family. "I thought it might be nice to go to the flower market today", I say. Every fourth Saturday, there's a travelling flower market that comes to town and I just so happened to plan my visit on the exact day they'd be here. Even though flowers are very cliché and girly, there's something about buying flowers and putting them out that warms a part of my chest.

"What a lovely idea, let me just go and get dressed", my mom says. I grab the newspaper off the table whilst I wait for her, idly flicking through the local news stories and announcements.

"Ready", my mom calls from the corridor and I get up and meet her by the front door. She's changed from a pair of brown smart trousers to black smart trousers with a cream blouse, a checkered scarf and a navy coat to ward off the chill outside. Mom closes the door behind us as we make our way to the market. With it being in the centre of town, it's about a half-hour walk from where my parents live. The cool, fresh air pinks my cheeks as we walk, my mom filling me in on all the recent drama between different neighbours. I nod along in the appropriate places, happy to let my mom speak as we pass row after row of perfect houses with perfectly mowed front gardens and wave at women in my mom's weekly book club. My mom's idea of a book club is vastly different from my own; where I would come prepared with all my thoughts and theories regarding character arcs and plot twists, my mom uses her book club as a chance to gossip with the neighbours over tea and cake. I guess as long as it makes her happy, who am I to begrudge her, right?

"Look at all those colours", my mom gushes as we arrive at the entrance to the flower market, "such a nice array of different flowers today". I nod along, eager to enter the market and immerse myself in the different smells and sights each flower provides.

"Oh look, Carol's over there", my mom coos, pointing out her best friend, "you go on and look at the flowers, I just need to go and catch Carol up on a few things", she smiles and ambles towards Carol. As she calls her name, Carol turns around and pulls her into a quick hug. And not two seconds later, they eagerly start talking, about what I can't be sure of. I take the time walking through isle after isle after isle, the deep orange and reds of autumn coming alive to me in the delicate flower petals, the beginnings of winter creeping in with the sprigs of holly and fern. I take a couple of photos, knowing the vibrant colours of the flowers will make for a captivating home screen on my phone and pick up a few different bunches to take home. I choose a gorgeous bunch of red roses, a red so dark it's almost black. The colour is so deep I feel like getting lost in it. Cliché as it might sound, red roses are my favourite flowers. I don't know what it is but there's something intoxicating about them; they are simple in their elegance but demand attention. What I wouldn't give to feel even a sliver of the audacity of a red rose.

Not that I need any more flowers; my apartment is already a veritable jungle of small and large leafy plants, dotted in random corners or edges of my shelves. My mom walks over just as I'm paying for my flowers and offers to buy them for me as a well done on my performance at uni.

"Thanks mom", I say as we head back home, and she waves away my gratitude as though the gesture is nothing.

"Do you want to stay for dinner before you head off", my mom says.

"Yeah sure, why not", it beats having to cook for myself for a change.

"Perfect, we're having chicken pie".

"Sounds great mom" and it really does. It's the perfect kind of dinner to go with the crisp autumn air outside.

The rest of the afternoon passes with relative ease. The three of us eat dinner together and my dad manages the entire meal without making a snide remark about my choice of work or university course. He even congratulates me on my good grades after my mom tells him how well I'm doing.

"We'll see you at Christmas", my dad says as he walks me out.

"See you then", I wave goodbye and walk to my car. For once, I leave their house relatively content, the flowers my mom bought me on the passenger seat beside me. Buckling in, I hope for good traffic and begin my journey home. Thankfully, it only takes me just over two hours to get home and I'm exhausted from spending the majority of the day in the car. I set about putting my roses in vases and dotting them around my apartment, the red a splash of colour against my neutral walls, then make quick work of getting ready for bed. Too tired to even read, I message my parents to tell them I got home okay before putting my phone on silent and getting into bed. It doesn't take long for sleep to find me once my head hits the pillow and I welcome the oblivion of sleep.

Chapter Twenty.

Paige

It's been seven days, one whole week, and I've heard nothing from Lawrence. Not to be one of those girls, but I can't help asking myself why hasn't he messaged me? And yeah, I could message him, but surely if he was really interested, he'd reach out first? I know it's silly to obsess so much over the few moments we've spent together, but I felt so at ease with Lawrence that I really did think it could be the start of something good. At least for a little while anyway. Oh well, I'm proud of myself for simply putting myself out there, rather than continuing to live in the cage of my own solitude. Even if the sting of rejection hurts more than I'd care to admit.

Despite checking my phone every few hours for a text that never comes through, the past week has flown by in a flurry of visiting my family, uni deadlines and overtime at work. Distraction is the best fix for an overactive mind. At least I have the day off today, which means spending the morning in bed, trying to coax myself from beneath my warm covers and the peace that sleep always brings. I spend the morning reading, getting lost between the pages of fictitious characters and unrealistic love stories, comforted by the characters that touch my life, if only for the time it takes me to get from one book to the next. Maybe it's my solitary lifestyle that causes such a fervour for reading, but the safety I find in between the lines of each fictional adventure is unlike anything the real world has ever been able to offer me. This is why the only thing I've ever been able to trust steadfastly is reading, because the only hurt it ever causes me is the kind that is second nature.

I hurt because a beloved character of mine is killed in a tragedy. I hurt because I don't agree with the way the author gives a villain, who doesn't deserve it, a brilliant redemption arch. I hurt because sometimes an author is able to put into words what I'm feeling, in ways even I cannot. I hurt because my own emotions only become expressible to me in the mouths of fictional characters. I hurt because none of the connections I make are ever real.

I hurt because it's never real.

But it's always there. No matter how many eons go by and civilisations that turn to dust, the desire for someone to pen their thoughts down on paper for any who will indulge them is ageless. It defies time.

That's why I can only ever truly rely on the escape of my books, the comfort and solace I find between pages, because how can it ever abandon me if it will outlive me?

It can't.

I'm so caught up in the pages of my book that I don't even realise the time. It's well past one in the afternoon by the time I even bother to get out of my bed, tearing myself away from the plot twist I can feel is on the cusp of being revealed. I tell myself to get up and run my few errands, with the promise of returning to my bed to read as soon as my tasks are complete. Maybe I'll even run and get a coffee on the way home, as a reward for simply forcing myself to endure life today. Name a better duo than a good book and coffee. I know I can't.

The weather is miserable again, rain misting the air with perpetual moisture. Not bothering to look my best, I head out in a baggy jumper and tracksuits, layering up to hide away from the dismal atmosphere outside. I take a slow walk to the post office, enjoying the cold air that weaves its way into my lunges, the dampness that clings to my eyelashes and skin. When the weather is this grey, the streets are pretty quiet, inhabited only by those who either can't drive, live for the drizzle, or want a change in pace from the boredom of the four brick walls that surround them. I walk in near solitude, smiling at the odd person who also happens to brave the misery, counting the cracks in the pavement beneath my feet as a way of passing time. It takes me no more than fifteen minutes to reach the post office, the sign on the door says open in a cheery shade of yellow.

I push the door open, immediately enveloped in a rush of warm air. Making my way to the counter, I rummage in my bag for the item I wish to return. Oh, the agony of buying online, you never can guarantee that what you order will in fact be what you desire. I guess that's the same with people too; just because we find someone attractive at first glance, doesn't mean our souls speak the same language. Instead, you could find someone who you have an insane physical connection to but they lack anything to make that connection more profound, more meaningful.

"I need to return this please, I have a QR code to scan for the return address", I smile at the woman behind the counter, recognising her face from my many trips to the post office.

"Sure thing, pass it over". With the simple click of a button, my label is printed, and my parcel is secreted away, ready to be returned to sender. The simplicity of modern technology at its finest. My only other order of business for the day is grabbing some food for dinner, so I make my way the short distance to the shops to get flour and macaroni for homemade mac and cheese later. With both the post office and dinner checked off my to-do list, I can comfortably allow myself to go straight back to bed without the guilt of doing nothing for the entire day.

But first, coffee.

The queue out the front door of the coffee shop is less than ideal, but the warm thoughts of coffee and a good read get my feet moving to the back of the queue before the practical voice in my head, that says I can make coffee at home, has even reared its ugly head. I'm hit first by the smell of coffee, then the cacophony of noises that ebb and flow as friends with loved ones and couples bicker at the seemingly inane. It didn't take long for the barista to make my coffee. Now one of the establishment's regulars, I no longer need to order, I just walk in and pay, my coffee sitting waiting for me on the side. This time, however, the queue is so long that after paying, I have to wait a good ten minutes before the rush has died down enough for the baristas to get to my order. I take the time to drink in my surroundings, in awe of the easy-going manner those around me seem to exude. I'd be lying if I said I wasn't envious of their ability to just jump into life. Of course, you never really know what is going on in someone else's head, but on the surface, all these strangers seem, if not happy, then content at the very least.

The man in front of me picks up his black americano, and I'm again reminded of Lawrence's eyes and their depth that seemed to go on forever. As the man walks away, I grab my own drink off the counter, excited again by the prospect of snuggling under my covers and reading. Because I am nothing if not a creature of habit and there's not enough money in the world to try and convince me otherwise.

The walk back home takes no time at all and my ability to jump back into bed even less so.

The second I open my book, I'm pulled back into the escapades of mythical creatures at war with their own kind and heartbreak so potent my own heart bleeds a little from the tragedy of it. I guess the closest thing to heartbreak I'll ever experience is the first-person accounts I read, since I'm too scared to let anyone close enough to cause my own heartbreak. And maybe it's that tragic thought, my own comfortableness with living so completely by myself, that compels me to put my book down and pick up my phone. Maybe it's that secret desire that burns like a tiny flame in my soul, that invisible teardrop of loneliness in my eye, that has my fingers typing away with little conscious thought. Maybe it's that voice in my head that started to yawn awake the first time I heard Lawrence speak, but before I can second guess myself, or change my mind, I take some initiative and message Lawrence first, because it's about time that I stopped letting the fear of rejection keep me from living.

Chapter Twenty-One

Lawrence

"Your inability to follow orders is becoming rather tiresome", Anchor doesn't so much as bother to look in my direction as he slams the door and prowls to his desk, where I stand patiently, readying for my verbal execution.

"I don't know what has gotten into you, but this little act of defiance will not go unpunished. We do not wait for souls to enter The Beyond. We are not humans. We do not offer comfort and companionship. We are ruthless followers of the Universe, whose sole purpose is to carry out the cosmic order, without question, without remorse". I stand like a penitent with my head bowed, arms stoically clasped together behind my back. Like the good little soldier that I'm expected to be. I listen to his diatribe, his verbal lashing, with the insouciance of one who has lost all meaning of himself. Of course, Anchor has every reason to rip me a new one. I was disobedient, impulsive, reckless. And yet, I cannot seem to muster up the appropriate feeling of guilt that shunning my responsibilities should evoke.

"Law, are you even listening to me?".

"Yes sir", lifting my head I meet his raging glare, willing my eyes void of anything other than loyal obedience.

"And what exactly do you have to say for yourself? I would say that this behaviour is exactly the kind of thing that one finds himself doing when looking to be stricken off, demoted to the lower services of this order".

Genuine fear hits my gut at his words, the first real thing I've felt other than boredom since I stepped foot in his office not ten minutes ago. Stricken off. Lower service. I cannot let that happen, cannot let my actions today result in Paige being reassigned.

She is mine.

"Nothing I can say can make up for my error, sir, but I can assure you it will not happen again". Whilst Anchor stares at me with blatant disdain burning in his eyes, I feel a faint buzzing in my pocket, alerting me to some notification on my phone. Not that I'm inclined to look at that meaningless piece of machinery often, but doing so now, in front of Anchor, would no doubt cement my demotion to the lower services of what I'm now seeing as a wretched order. It hits me how hopeless hating what you do for a living truly feels like; how isolating it is to have absolutely zero belief in the thing that you're expected to do, day in, day out. I don't bother trying to disguise the sigh that escapes my lips.

Finally deigning to acknowledge me, Anchor warns me that I'm on "very thin ice" and nods towards the door, a swift dismissal I am eager to accept.

Walking out the door, closing it delicately behind me, I pull my phone out of my pocket, searching for any temporary distraction. A smile tugs on my lips, despite knowing it shouldn't, as I see the text message from Paige light up my screen.

'The other night was fun.'

It reads, nothing more. And I couldn't agree more. The last week has been a practice of sheer mortal determination not to message Paige, to see her again, to get to know her in ways my role as a Reaper forbids me. Which is why I've stayed away, because the other night stirred something in me that goes so much deeper than me simply reaping a soul: I want to know her soul, be part of her life. Not stop her from existing. So, I thought keeping my distance would ensure my focus on my mission, rather than being distracted by her.

I click on her message, leaving it on seen for now, battling my duties against my internal confusion. My meeting with Anchor was my last official duty of the day. As a Reaper, you never completely sign off, but I have nothing imminent for the rest of the evening, I am just on call for any calamities that may arise. I find myself almost wishing for tragedies on occasion; it's so hard to find things to fill my time, I don't know how humans do it on such a regular basis. My research of them during my training days has allowed me to discover various literature and art forms, some being mildly interesting, others seemingly a waste of time. None of which draw my interest this evening.

With nothing on my mind other than that text message burning a hole in my pocket, I decide a night-time walk is in order. I don't bother stopping by my room to grab a jacket, since the tribulations of maintaining a steady temperature don't faze us Reapers. I go straight from Anchor's office out the front door.

The streets around HQ are fairly rudimentary, grey, concrete streets lined with redbrick offices and small terrace houses struggling for room on the pavement. Not wanting to run into anyone, I make my way towards the small park located fifteen minutes away from HQ, the dreary weather and late time of day mean I cross paths with hardly a soul. I know I think it often, but the night really is a place of calm, of peacefulness. Perhaps it is because it reminds me of where all humans eventually go; into an endless nothingness.

As predicted, the park is empty, occupied only by myself and a lone magpie perched on the metal chain of a swing. What is the rhyme that humans use with magpies? One for sorrow? I'd say that is fairly accurate to my current predicament. Needing some time to think, I take a seat on the swing, my mind circling around thoughts of Paige as though she is the sun I was made to orbit. And although the Egyptian pyramids, with the arid climate and endless sand, is my normal place of refuge, tonight, sitting in this ordinary park feels right in a way the wonders of human architecture don't. Perhaps the time with Paige has already rubbed off on me more than I thought, if I can so suddenly find comfort in this mundane patch of grass and rusty swing. But I do. And I don't know what to do about that.

My legs are so long they stretch out awkwardly in front of me as I let my body swing from side to side. My mind keeps returning to the text from Paige, the real reason I'm sitting in this park. It is not a coincidence that it's only a five-minute walk from her home. I'm sitting here because I want to be close to her. The swing creaks as I move it pointlessly to the side, the movement just jarring enough in the stillness of the night that it's almost exhilarating. And maybe I need some kind of personal jarring from the monotony that I have accepted over the centuries. As painful as it will be, maybe getting to know Paige is my due for being so diligent, so unquestioning in my role. I know time is running out, the finite minutes of Paige's life trickling to a close as I sit here and contemplate the rigidity of my own existence. Perhaps I shouldn't care at all. But I do and it's too late now anyway. The desire to know her became inevitable the moment her beautiful blue eyes lit up the gloom of the cemetery.

I stretch my neck, made uncomfortable from carrying the weight of all my problems and decide that getting to know Paige isn't even just about me anymore. It's about making sure she learns how to live and feel alive before I become the villain in her story and take it away.

I know all humans hate the bad guys, but maybe they've never considered that their wretched actions aren't a result of their character but are simply the demands of an unforgiving Universe.

Chapter Twenty-Two

Lawrence

It's early morning before I know it, my back in muted agony at having sat hunched on this swing for the last few hours. The sun peaks behind the clouds, too shy in the cobwebs of the night to appear in its entirety. I made the decision last night to give Paige a life that makes her feel alive. And that's exactly what I'm going to do.

Leaving the park behind, the grass soft with condensation, I take a right, walking towards Paige's house. If I've learned something from the few films I've watched over the years, it's that girls like to be wanted; they want to know that there's someone out there whose day is made better simply by being in their presence. And I think the male population has failed Paige somewhat; her reserved, almost anxious disposition not only wrought from the horrors her own mind conjures up, but perhaps from the way the world, and those in it, have let her down. I know I owe her nothing, my only job in her life is to take her soul and ferry it on. But I have this aching feeling in my chest that I can't put into words and the thought of never getting to know Paige is almost crippling. I think the only cure for this is to know her as much as I can, in the short time I am offered.

By the time my thoughts have slowed, I'm walking around the corner to the street Paige lives on. My feet carry me the rest of the way until I'm standing outside her door, hand poised to knock. It's only now that I'm outside that I realise how creepy this might seem – I didn't reply to her message but now I'm outside her front door like her own personal stalker. She did say she's watched *Scream* a dozen times though, so perhaps she finds Billy's psychotic tendencies somewhat endearing. There's nothing to be done now other than taking the plunge. I knock on the door three times, the wood smooth beneath my knuckles. It feels like a lifetime waiting for the door to open. As I'm just about to turn away, labelling this mission a fruitless endeavour, never to be repeated, the door creaks softly open.

Chapter Twenty-Three

Paige

Despite my earlier bravado of seizing life by the horns and putting myself out there, it backfired with my text being left on seen. I waited all of ten minutes last night for a response from Lawrence before deciding to get a grip of myself and go to sleep. But I still couldn't escape the sinking disappointment of waking up to an empty screen, devoid of any notifications.

No message is a message. So even if I didn't get the response I wanted, I can move forward now and forget about him.

But at least I did it. And although I went to bed a little dejected, I've woken up feeling refreshed. I forgot to shut my curtains last night, so the early morning sun trickles into my bedroom, a soft kiss of warmth to welcome me into the day. Other than a few bits of uni work to complete, I have the day mostly to myself again which will be nice. I think people underestimate the power of alone time. There's something grounding and relaxing in being able to spend a whole day by yourself.

I brush my teeth, get of out my pyjamas and head downstairs to make a coffee. If I don't have coffee within the first hour of getting up, my day feels incomplete from the get-go. It's also nice to have a routine; without the consistency of a daily routine, my life seems to just turn into chaos. And that doesn't mean to say that I can't be flexible, I'm just more resistant to it than the average person.

I treated myself a while ago to a Nespresso machine and life since just hasn't been the same. It allows me to romanticise coffee more than I already do. Choosing a flavoured pod, I put it in the machine and go heat some milk whilst the coffee makes itself. The smell of coffee fills my little kitchen, the whirring of the machine almost hypnotic in its gentle hum. Just as I'm pouring the milk, the white eddying and swirling with the rich brown, I hear a knock at my door. Well, not one knock, but three.

Tap. Tap. Tap.

I haven't ordered anything over the last few days so I'm not expecting a delivery. Apprehension is like a snake in my belly, creeping around and setting my nerves on edge. It's awfully early for anyone to be visiting and I'm tempted to leave the door unanswered, but curiosity pulls my feet towards the hall, the soft scuff of my slippers the only sound. I give myself a quick once over in the hallway mirror – not my best look but also, by far not my worst. With a shrug, I pull open the door a fraction and peer beyond to see who is outside.

I blink. And blink again, unsure if what I'm seeing is accurate or if I've finally started to lose my mind. Lawrence stands in front of me, his body angled slightly away in retreat. He wears nothing but a black shirt and black jeans, the concept of a jacket or coat clearly lost on him. He has smudges under his eyes, tired circles begging for the relief of sleep, the only visible flaw to his otherwise good looks. I fumble for something to say, not used to surprise encounters so early in the morning. Or at all, if I'm being honest.

"Hi", I breathe, both embarrassed and intrigued by his presence outside my home. I glance up and find him looking at me, and if I had more self-confidence than I currently possess, I would say the look in his eyes is one of hunger, like he could devour me whole and it still wouldn't be enough.

"I had fun the other night too", Lawrence says, still looking at me with such intensity that I break eye contact first and look at the floor, the spot behind his left shoulder, anywhere but directly at him. "So much so that I thought we could do something again" he continues, "today if you're free?". He stands there expectantly, his hands in his pockets, a smile slowly creeping onto his face, a little taunt that dares me to accept.

"I - I don't know what to say", I stumble, trying to decide if this kind of spontaneity is exciting or derailing.

"Well, you could start by saying yes and we can go from there". He leans towards me, resting his hand on the edge of my doorframe like it belongs to him. The cool scent of night floats towards me on an errant morning breeze, soothing my frayed edges, instilling in me a sense of calm I've never quite felt before. He's almost cocky in the way he looks at me, now leaning wholly against my doorframe, creeping into my personal space with the kind of dominance I find too intriguing to ignore.

"I have some uni work that I need to get done this morning but other than that I'm all yours". I cringe, realising what I've just said. I always do this, say something that can be construed in a way other than how I meant it and end up wanting the ground to swallow me whole. But Lawrence ignores my wince, the flush of embarrassment I can feel inching over my cheeks.

"Just how I want you to be", winking he pushes off the doorframe, taking me in in my entirety. He pulls off winking in a way most males are inept; it's an effortless gesture, understated, all mischief and seduction, not arrogant or debauched. Intriguing. If I wasn't going to say yes before, there's no way I can say no now.

"I'll come back around one then if that gives you enough time?"

"Sounds good to me", I nod. Still baffled, Lawrence tips his head at me, sliding his hands into his jean pockets, he turns around and heads back down the walkway. Even though I watch him walk the entire way, retreating down my road with the ease of someone with nowhere else to be, it's like his half there-half not. One minute I can see him as clear as day, the black of his clothes standing out against the tired grey pavement beneath his feet. And the next minute, his black outline seems to wash away, blending in with the trees that line the street. Strange. Shutting my door, I shake my head and go back inside. I heat my coffee up and get my head down, determined to get as much work done as possible before Lawrence returns.

***

I spend a couple of hours going over the nervous system and how transmissions are sent between synapses. The human body is pretty fascinating. There are so many processes going on within our bodies every second that we don't even consciously think about. Being able to breathe is second nature for us but the minute we start to focus on it, it becomes too much for our minds to bear and we feel frazzled, off-centre. Like in yoga practices, yes, they tell you to focus on your breathing because it grounds you, but the second you want to go back to breathing unconsciously, it becomes hard to find the natural rhythm of it again. We don't give our bodies the credit they deserve most of the time. I study it because it makes me appreciate things that much more.

The clock on my laptop tells me it's half twelve, so I have just under half an hour to make myself presentable. Not that I ever do much in the way of getting ready. I'm pretty low maintenance. I don't wear make-up because I'd much rather spend those extra twenty minutes of a morning in bed, than contouring my face to the point where I no longer resemble myself. And even though most of the time I find myself to be average at best, the odd times I wear a dab of lipstick or touch of mascara, I feel outside of myself. Uncomfortable. Which is why I generally settle for my natural face than feel like an imposter hiding behind make-up.

Getting ready consists of me changing out of my slouchy clothes into something that shows I've made a little more effort. I opt for mom jeans and a long-sleeved bodysuit, perhaps two of the most understated items in the history of the female wardrobe. Not to turn this into a tirade about fashion, but there's something about a bodysuit that's not only comfortable but also classy; it makes you feel put together despite the simplicity of the outfit itself.

Happy with the clothes I've got on, I fold my tracksuits back into the wardrobe and go downstairs to await Lawrence's arrival. Not knowing how to fill the next ten minutes with anything meaningful, I scroll through Instagram, mindlessly taking in the exotic lives of celebrities and pictures of food acquaintances of mine have had for lunch. Riveting. It's hard not to fall into the trap of comparison sometimes, scrutinising the way my life seems lacking or different from the on-screen personas people portray to the digital world through their phones. I think that's why I avoid looking where possible, because if I refuse to give these unrealistic entities the time of day, then I can't compare myself to this over-distorted misrepresentation of adult life. Just as I finish watching a video of someone painting their nails, I hear that soft knock knock knock on my door.

"Ready?", Lawrence asks as I open the door. I nod as I lock up behind me, curious to see how this day will play out.

"Lead the way", I nod. Lawrence takes my hand and ushers me down the walkway, into the mild sun overhead and possibility beyond.

Chapter Twenty-Four

Paige

We walk in silence for the first five minutes. My feet carry me aimlessly, following a straight path down the road to wherever it is that Lawrence is taking us. Part of me wants to ask where we're going and what we're doing, but the other part of me is screaming to just be wild and see where the day takes us. It isn't every day that I'm given the opportunity to spend time with someone who looks like they've walked straight off the set of a Hollywood movie. I refuse to waste my breath panicking over being unable to control the day, and instead make sure I enjoy what the Universe has sent my way.

"So, I thought we could start the day with coffee, and then go from there". Lawrence glances over at me, just at the same time the sun decides to hide behind the clouds. The low light of the morning makes his eyes even darker, a black hole so dangerously intoxicating, that for a moment, for just one small second, I forget what it means to breathe. I can feel it, some indefinable tug between us: he is gravity and I am falling hopelessly towards the earth, unable to resist the natural laws of science. He could be both the worst and best thing to ever happen to me. Just looking into his eyes awakens something in me, a quiet yearning that I've smothered for too long for fear that the world will find me lacking. And even if this is the last time I see him, I know I won't be able to put the veritable genie back in the box; it is outside of myself now, this desire to be adventurous, to live. And how can I capture life back into myself when the world is so hungry for every drop of our existence?

Realising I haven't answered Lawrence, I smile back at him, too busy drowning in his eyes to notice the ground beneath my feet. Too busy to stop myself from tripping over the cracked pavement, my shoe catching on the upturned corner, arms flailing like a mad woman to help regain my balance. Even despite pinwheeling my arms in a frenzy to regain my equilibrium, the floor starts to look closer than it did two minutes ago. I cringe, waiting for the painful thud of my face hitting the concrete, my pride and dignity in shreds along the road. As I'm preparing for the impact, my eyes clenched in anticipation, I feel a firm but gentle grip on my arm and then my waist. I blink, confused. It takes my brain a few seconds to realise that Lawrence's grip on my waist saved me from both a painful and embarrassing fall. We stand still for a moment, his hand still on my waist, his mouth open as if he's about to speak. Too embarrassed, I don't allow him the chance. Instead, I utter a quick thank you, moving just out of reach of his hands, now empty and hovering in the air as if without a purpose.

"Coffee sounds perfect to me", pretending as though the past two minutes didn't occur, I continue walking, hoping Lawrence will take my lead on the situation and follow. And it isn't just humiliation that spurs me onwards, my eyes now fixed obsessively on the pavement to ensure no other mishaps occur. But for those few precious moments when his hands were on my skin and his eyes were pouring into my soul, I felt that stirring of longing again, this time so potent and raw that the possibility of ignoring it feels like ignoring the blistering sun in a scorching desert: impossible and painful. I sneak a glance over at Lawrence, hopeful that I might find the same confusion I feel inside myself written bright as day on his handsome face. Instead, it's devastatingly blank, a frozen lake of passivity, as unaffected by me as a wolf undisturbed by a sparrow.

Just like that, I can't breathe again, the stupidity of my own heart and capacity to romanticise the world, once again leaving reality a dull grey blur in comparison to the world and desires conjured by my own mind.

We turn left instead of carrying straight on, veering from the route to the closest coffee shop. I look to Lawrence in silent question, the action alone enough to elicit a response.

"I thought it would be nice to try somewhere new today", he winks at me, as if knowing my penchant for routine, the ease and comfort of a familiar setting.

"As long as the coffee is nice, I don't mind where we go". And I really hope it is nice because there's nothing worse than a disappointing coffee, even if my standards for coffee are pretty low in the eyes of any coffee connoisseur out there. A friend at uni once told me that 'proper' coffee is made from beans with fruity undertones and that the coffee beans used in big chains like Costa or Starbucks are barely coffee in comparison. But I have to disagree. And maybe that makes me a fraud, an imposter who likes the idea of what coffee represents, the image it exudes to the world, the feeling I get when it scalds the back of my throat, rather than the taste of the thing itself, but coffee without syrup or sugar, or with the acrid notes of fruit, just aren't worth my time. Drinking coffee isn't just gulping down the caffeine it barely provides, it's an experience that one indulges themselves in.

"I've been here a few times with a friend of mine to catch up. The coffee is good and it's pretty undiscovered which makes talking easy in the quiet atmosphere." I can't deny that his words have left me intrigued, curious to see the place that has somehow enticed him. He pauses outside what looks to be a renovated semi-detached house, the front wall knocked out and replaced with floor-to-ceiling stained glass windows. Lawrence reaches the door and opens it, beckoning me inside with a brush of his hand against my lower back. I'd be lying if a tiny part of me doesn't sigh with contentment at that contact, small though it may be. As I walk inside, the colour of the windows is refracted like fireworks over the walls, the sun hitting the glass at just the right angle to make the entire place look like a dancing fireplace. Words fail me as I drink it all in. The wood floor beneath my feet is rich and worn; matching wooden tables line the back two walls, with smaller, rectangular tables dotted throughout the rest of the open space. Hand-dyed rugs of varying colours and patterns are scattered along the floor, adding an extra layer of comfort to the place that makes it feel welcoming and familiar, even though I've never been here before. The lighting is understated, the place lit up mostly by the colours of the window and yellow overhead lights dotted sparingly throughout. Lawrence was right, this place holds its own sort of charm, a siren calling all her would-be lovers' home. That's what the place feels like. Like a haven in a storm of human activity, this place is calm, it beats and breathes at a tempo outside of the bustle of everyday life. It's tranquil.

"This place is - it's", again I struggle to put into words how peaceful and intriguing it is. Lawrence smiles at me as if knowing what I want to say, despite words failing me.

"I know", he nods, making his way towards the counter. 'Caramel latte?', he asks, indicating the chalkboard menu behind the till. I'm suddenly hit with a sense of déjà vu, taken back to the first time we shared coffee. Mischief dances in Lawrence's eyes as if he's thinking of the same thing.

"Yes please, I'll get this coffee though, since you got the last one", I edge in front of him, getting closer to the till so I can put the order in and pay before he does.

"Absolutely not Paige, I'll get the coffee, you go get a seat". And I don't know if it's hearing my name on his lips, or the sheer demand in his tone when he says it, but I find myself nodding along subconsciously, my body drifting towards a small table tucked away in the back, nestled between two large fabric armchairs. I sit and wait whilst he orders the coffee, not noticing much of anything other than his husky voice over the background noise of coffee machines and hushed chit chat. Even though we've done this before, shared quiet conversation over coffee, I don't mind it one bit. And not just because I'm a stickler for habits, but because spending time with Lawrence feels natural, in a way other aspects of life so rarely seem to be.

Lawrence walks over with my coffee in his hand, his other hand painfully empty. He sets it down in front of me, the heart-shaped design of the milk a good indication of a well-seasoned barista.

"Here you go, I'll just be two secs", he nods towards the counter where the barista is making his coffee.

"That's okay, no problem, I can wait". And what I don't say is that I could wait forever, because sitting here in this place with him seems like an escape; a microcosm of suspended reality, emersed within, but completely separate from, the world outside. And what I wouldn't give to hold on to this feeling for eternity.

I think I would give my life for it, for this silence, this stillness, without a second thought.

Chapter Twenty-Five

Lawrence

I walk back over, black coffee in hand, and can't help but memorise every line of Paige's face. The soft curve of her ear hidden underneath her hair, the gentle shape of her lips, the foggy expression in those pure blue eyes, as if her thoughts are a chain around her neck, dragging her down. She picks up her mug and takes a sip of her drink, her whole body outwardly sighing in satisfaction, her tongue tracing her lips, languidly savouring every last drop. What would it feel like to have her lips on mine, to know her body intimately? The thought pops unbidden into my head, so intrusive and unexpected that I almost stumble as I place my coffee on the table between us. Stumble, because the notions of such a thing is so inherently human that it should be foreign to me. Should be, but isn't – at least not where Paige is concerned.

"Almost spilt your coffee there", she smiles up at me, and fuck if it doesn't make me hate myself that little bit more. I shake my head, smiling back at her, falling into easy conversation about nothing and everything all at once. She tells me about her uni work, and listening to her passion, the enthusiasm with which she speaks about her interests is enthralling. She is at first quiet and reserved, but there's a fire behind her eyes that rises to the surface when she speaks about things that mean something to her. I can't help being a little envious. Yes, from the outside she perhaps lives a rather uneventful life, keeping to herself, her work, and her books, rather than partying her nights away, losing herself in the touches of others. But it doesn't mean there isn't life inside her. She knows what she likes and there's something fiercely compelling about that, even if her proclivity for staying inside with herself robs her of the chance to see what the human world can truly offer her. But I'm hoping I will change that, show her what the world could be like, should the Universe have granted her the timeline to do so.

"Could you not see yourself living forever?", I ask her, the brevity of her timeline a ghost hovering over my shoulder.

"I couldn't think of anything worse. I can't imagine myself living for fifty years, let alone a hundred or another thousand after that".

"That's", I pause, unsure of how to express what her words have evoked, "that's sad". And sad doesn't even begin to cover the extent of what rages inside of me, taunting me, but too unknown for me to lock down.

She doesn't say anything else, but the potent emotion in her eyes tells me enough of the thoughts spiralling around in her head. *Now you know what it feels like to be in my head. I can barely picture being alive each time I get out of bed, to think of having to do this thing we call life for eternity, would be living torture.* Her eyes practically yell the words into my head. And a sick part of me is almost grateful that she struggles so intensely, because it means that maybe taking her life will be a small mercy for her. What a bastard I am to feel relief at robbing her of the chance to change her mind, to grow into herself and out of her neurosis.

She clears her throat, tilting her head back as she drains the last of her coffee. That sadness has settled in her eyes again, a thick cloak of despondency, drawing her out of her surroundings and into herself.

"Ready for the next part of the day?", I nod towards the door. Not waiting for a response, I grab the finished drinks and return the mugs to the counter, ambling towards the front door and streets outside. Paige trails after me with the reluctance of an abused dog, not wanting to be left behind, but scared of what will happen if she follows.

"My car is just around the corner, the next place we're going is too far to get to on foot". She nods as if only half interested, her eyes anywhere but on my face. Her disinterest makes me question whether she wants to continue what would be the equivalent of a date if I were human and allowed to partake in such things.

"Unless you'd rather leave the day here", I blurt, her silence compelling me to fill the empty space with words, begging for validation, for any small approval. She hesitates and my stomach drops, ready for her dismissal. And I suppose it will be a good thing, a relief. That way I can go back to my job as her Reaper and she can resume her title as my charge, a distant soul whose life I have no investment in, other than in those final moments where I will carry her to The Beyond.

"No, I want to see what else you have planned", and the smile she gives me lights something akin to joy in my chest. I nod at her, trying valiantly to contain my relief and guilt as I lead her down the road, towards the side street where my car is parked. Paige gasps, a barely audible intake of breath that has my head whipping to the side so quickly I'm surprised I don't give myself whiplash.

"What is it?".

"I don't know what I was expecting, but I didn't expect you to drive such a beaten up, worn down little car", she laughs, as if the idea of me in that metal contraption is an absurdity of the highest calibre. Little does she know it's a leftover token from my last charge. "You're just so broody and mysterious that I thought your car would be", she pauses, as if searching the entire Universe for the right word, "elegant?". She laughs again, her quiet giggle giving way to something more obnoxious and less delicate, erupting out of her like fire from a hot air balloon, in fits and bursts.

"Well, I'm glad my choice of car is amusing to you", I wink, opening the passenger side and beckoning her in. After shutting her door, I get behind the wheel, fiddling around with the temperamental radio until I find a station that plays with minimal interference.

"Where are we off to?", I can barely hear her question over the sputter of the engine roaring to life, the whir of the wheels as they slowly move over the tarmacked road a reassuring hum in the background.

"Since the weather is nice, I thought we could head up to The Hills and go for a walk". What I don't say is that there's a small night life nestled in between the valleys that I'm hoping I can take Paige to, if we decide to stay that long. Just so I can unleash that fire within her for the world to see, so she can unleash herself with no hesitation, to be in the moment and just let herself go.

"I like that, being outside can be refreshing", she nods at me.

"The drive is a little while away, but it will be worth it once we get there". I change gears, accelerating faster as I move onto a main road, away from the buildings and bustle of every day and out into the open. Concrete and grey turns to green and countryside, the trees a blurring mosaic of colours outside the window, Paige a calming presence at my side as her gaze roams over the scenery. We don't speak, but the silence is personable, soothing, a warm blanket wrapping around our bodies like the comfort of an old friend. The music is secondary to the hum of Paige's body, my Reaper sense so in tune with her soul, that it is music to me in and of itself. Right now, her soul is a quiet thing, a low hum of anticipation that she is completely unaware of.

We drive like this for miles, content to watch the road go by as the car speeds over the miles it takes to reach The Hills on the outside of town, the silence an invisible thread between our two bodies. And in this moment, if there were one thing I could ask the Universe for, it would be to freeze time, to grant me the privilege of basking in this tentative solitude for more than a few minutes. I can't help but yearn for the fulfilment of humanity, the joys and sorrows that come in abundance, to know intimately what it means to be human in all its blessings and calamities. But in this car, with the wind swaying the metal almost ferociously, and the white noise of music and our combined breathing, I almost feel it, that place I fit. I almost find that place I am meant to be. With Paige, and nowhere else. I can imagine the idea of loving her and the world around us, appreciating what I have because it is doomed to end, as all human experiences are.

What will become of me when she is no longer? When she no longer grants me this glimmer of humanity? The thought unsettles me for the rest of the drive, disturbing that transitory calm that slipped through my fingers like the sands of time through an invisible net.

What will become of me?

Chapter Twenty-Six

Paige

The drive feels both infinite and no time at all, the blurs of the scenery and road beneath the car a calming presence. After we reached the stretch of road that leads to The Hills, Lawrence parks up and we walk the rest of the way. All done in silence, content to be in each other's presence. I think that's the truest form of intimacy - being comfortable enough not to have to fill the silence with meaningless conversation, but letting your energies, your souls, speak in languages unfathomable to our human ears.

We continue the trek in companionable silence and I can't help taking secret glances at Lawrence. He seems different out in the countryside, younger, more vulnerable, like the fresh air and majesty of nature are incomprehensible to him, despite what his eyes show him. There's a small light in his eyes, as though he's in awe of the world around him, as though he has never quite taken in the moment the way he seems to be doing now, with me, the verdant hills and untamed brambles around us, his first glimpse into the wilderness that life really is.

'It's beautiful, isn't it?', I ask, standing atop the lowest peak, my eyes towards the horizon. Lawrence sidles up beside me and I can feel the whisper of his breath on my ear as he looks out towards the rolling hills and setting sun. He doesn't answer me with words but just gives me a slow nod, the emotion in his eyes almost knocking me over. And it isn't awe that now floats to the surface, but pain, a sense of hopelessness I've only ever seen reflected in the mirror. He looks like he's lost something he never even had to begin with. It's puzzling. Is nature really that dear to him? He opens his mouth to say something but then closes it again. Before I can say anything else, before I can try and coax out of him what he seems so desperate yet reluctant to say, he starts walking again, powerful strides up the hill as though running away from the words left unsaid.

I chase after him, the wind blowing my hair to pieces as I practically jog to be by his side again. The soft crunch of the grass underfoot is the only sound around us, the birds and crickets silent as though quieted by some unknowable force. I hear more than see Lawrence's mouth move, still in that silent battle of wills to voice the thoughts swirling around his head. Up ahead, there is a small, crumbling ruin, the last goodbye of an ancient world. Covered in crawling ivy, the stone walls of the long-forgotten church seem to shimmer slightly in the last rays of the sun. I'm not religious in the sense that I go to church every Sunday or pray fervently to a higher power, but our existence is too complex to have happened by chance; the strings that pull us towards our future are too sentient to be a consequence of a hurtling meteor or cosmic shift eons ago. It's nice to think something is watching over us, even if it's the same something that pulls us towards our end, each second ticking away until we have no seconds left.

In the middle of the stone walls sits a small fountain, filled to the brim with rainwater that has trickled in from the gaping mouth that should have been the roof. I make my way towards the fountain, dipping my fingers in the murky water and watching as ripples spread from my dancing fingertips. If only I had a penny so I could make a wish, not that I'd even know what to wish for. I close my eyes instead, looking within myself for something I yearn for, but nothing jumps out at me. I guess it's hard to know what you want when at times you don't even know who you are. I sigh, opening my eyes and almost jump back in surprise. Lawrence stands not two feet in front of me, on the other side of the fountain, his hand outstretched towards me, about to graze my cheek. His hand lingers in mid-air, trembling as if waging a war, as though the mere thought of touching me is both a blessed relief and his downfall.

"I wish I had a penny to make a wish", I laugh, breaking the silence and bringing Lawrence back into himself.

"I don't think I need a penny to get what I want". He moves around the fountain to stand directly in front of me, his hand cupping my cheek, the indecision from moments ago gone. Before I even know what to make of it, Lawrence's lips are on mine, feather-light, as though he is scared of breaking some unspoken thing between us. He brushes his thumb along my cheekbone almost reverently, my heart in my throat as he leans in closer, my lower back now delicately pushed against the fountain's lip, Lawrence's arms a cage around me.

He pulls away, his eyes searching mine for validation. Instead of words, I pull him back in, content to speak with our bodies, my lips moving across his desperately, letting the movement of my tongue tell him of my intrigue and excitement. It's my turn to pull away and I trace my fingertip across his lips, echoing the path my mouth just travelled. Surprise, and something I can't quite put my finger on, dances behind Lawrence's eyes, gone before I can puzzle it out.

"There's a B&B, on the other side of the hill. I thought we could take a look, get some food and maybe stay the night. Two rooms of course", he adds quickly. I nod, too dazed to summon any words. He nods back, stepping out of arms reach and makes his way out of the crumbling stone church. The sun must have set whilst we were kissing because now the sky is a dusky grey, the temperature dropping as the night closes in. From where we stand, I can't see the tell-tale signs of a pub, no smoke from a chimney, no chatter from the resident drinkers inside. It must be too far away for my poor human eyes to detect. Body tired from the walk up here and the adrenaline of kissing Lawrence having sapped my energy, I begrudgingly start the descent down the other side of the hill, the wind a soft caress against my face, Lawrence a steady presence by my side.

***

A clunky bell chimes as Lawrence opens the door to the pub and ushers me inside. I unceremoniously wipe my trainers on the mat at the entrance and stand to the side of the door, Lawrence doing the same. A chubby, pink-cheeked lady approaches us from across the room, an easy smile on her face.

"What can I get you", she chirps, the rural undertones of her accent like a slap in the face compared to Lawrence's crisp, unaccented voice.

"A table for two please and two rooms for the night".

"Of course, follow me. I'll just need a name to put on the room, what shall it be?", she asks as she guides us across the room full of bubbling conversation, to a small wooden table nestled before the large open fireplace.

We each thank her as we take our seats and Lawrence gives his name to add to the rooms.

"Lawrence, why, that's a nice name, can't say I know a Lawrence myself", she laughs to herself. "And I'll just need a last name as well please". Her words echo into the silence, heavy stones falling into a sea of quiet. She looks at Lawrence expectantly, the appropriate time it should have taken him to answer her now bordering on rude and awkward. I follow her gaze, taking in Lawrence's wide eyes, the awkward movement of his lips as he fumbles for something to say. I pull up short, scanning my memory for a last name that Lawrence has never given me. He never gave me one.

"It's Grimm", at last, the words almost fly out of his mouth. He takes a sip of water as if washing his mouth of the words.

"Well, Mr Grimm, it's a pleasure to have you stay with us. I'll go fetch some menus and I'll come right back". And just like that, the cloud of awkward tension dissipates under the hostess' amiable smile, Lawrence relaxing back into himself whilst I scan the rest of the room, if only to give myself a reprieve from looking into those depthless eyes.

As expected, the place is bustling with activity, everyone getting ready to hunker down for the night, sharing drinks and memories from the warmth of inside, sheltering from the cold winds so common in the valley of The Hills. In the corner by the door, a group of men are playing darts, cheers of delight and cries of frustration erupting every few minutes when someone hits the bullseye or misses the board completely. Two tables down from ours, a couple sit enjoying each other's company; a candle in the middle of the table, hands stretched towards hands, as they share a gentle kiss. I look away quickly from the emotion that passes between them, a sharp pang of jealousy and longing snakes through my gut at the connection they share. Could I ever have that? Even if I could, is that what I really want? Who am I kidding, of course I do. All anyone ever really wants is a place to belong, someone they belong to, no matter how hard they might try and deny it.

"On the house", a pretty waitress sets down two glasses, filled precariously to the brim with pale yellow liquid, a wedge of lemon clinging to the side, a colourful paper straw standing in the centre. I look at Lawrence quizzically; he must have ordered them whilst I was people-watching. But his subtle head shake tells me he didn't order them either.

"It's limoncello spritz, the drink of the night. All guests get a free drink as a welcome", the waitress informs us, amusement twinkling in her eyes at our looks of confusion. "Enjoy", she winks and saunters off towards the bar, appreciative glances from both the male and female patrons following her every step.

Lawrence eyes the drink sceptically, the condensation from the glass dropping onto his open palm as he picks it up.

"Cheers", Lawrence winks, taking a hesitant sip. I do the same, the liquid a cold burst of flavour as the alcohol burns its way down my throat. I cough, not expecting it to be so strong. Just one sip and I feel like my head is already in the clouds, my mind slowly losing itself to the oblivion of alcohol.

I take another sip, enjoying the fizz of the bubbles down my throat, my body tingling as the warmth of the alcohol spreads over my body.

"Cheers", I salute Lawrence with my glass, eager and somewhat anxious to see how the evening will unfold. The ease in which the drink goes down and the light-headedness I'm already starting to feel suggests that tonight could fly before my eyes, a fleeting memory too quick for my senses to hold onto. I take another sip of my drink, the glass already half empty, and settle in to see what the night holds.

Chapter Twenty-Seven

Lawrence

I think I was able to hide the surprise and apprehension at my first sip of alcohol better than I did when trying to think of a last name. I came up with the only thing I could, an ode to the job I now loathe, and perhaps a hidden warning for Paige of the calamity I bring towards her. The alcohol tasted both better and worse than imagined. I hid my wince as it trickled down my throat, the effects of alcohol hindered by my inhuman body.

Across from me, Paige's drink is already half finished, her cheeks now a soft pink from both the warmth of the fire and heat of the alcohol. They make the blue of her eyes stand out that much brighter and I can feel myself getting drunk just off the sight of her, her appearance more intoxicating than any drink could possibly be. As she drinks from her glass, her tongue runs over her lips, catching any wayward drops of liquid. And I don't know what this feeling is, but if I had to guess, I'd liken it to desire, a slow simmering of my blood, an insistent tug towards Paige so strong I struggle to ignore it. Like earlier in that old church, despite my better judgement, I couldn't help but trace her lips with mine, needing to explore the taste of her mouth; needing to know what the mere act of kissing feels like. In trying to help Paige live a little before I end her life, that same desire to live seems to be awakening in me also. And fuck if that doesn't spell trouble. *But what is it that humans say? Carpe Diem?*

The idea of food forgotten, I push back my chair, extending my hand to Paige in what I hope is a friendly gesture. She cocks her head to the side, a silent question in those dazzling eyes. And I find myself lost in them again; swimming in an endless pool of Paige, her desires and insecurities bubbling to the surface like the drink bubbling in her hand.

"There's a room in the back with music", I nod towards the door to the left of the bar. Paige hesitates, uncertainty washing out the freeing relief the alcohol seemed to give her. What I don't say is that I only know of this room because of a past soul I had to reap there.

"I don't really dance", she says, her head timidly avoiding eye contact, retreating back into the cage she has made around herself.

"Neither do I". I grin and grab her hand, coaxing her out of her seat and into the slow trickle of people all now heading towards the room in the back. I pull Paige up beside me and allow myself the little pleasure of guiding her with a steady hand on her lower back. I can't seem to stop doing that, making small gestures of contact, almost as if to assure myself she is really there. It is unheard of for a Reaper to even think about these kinds of things, but here I am, eased by the solidity of Paige's warm skin beneath my hand like a nervous dog, whose trembling is only quieted by their owner's steady presence.

The music room is full of half-drunk patrons, some sitting, some moving along to the song the musicians are playing. I lead Paige into a quiet corner, watching her watch with rapt fixation; couples and friends dance together both elegantly and clumsily with big smiles on their faces as if the only thoughts they have are of being happy. I can see Paige's foot tapping along to the music, the only visible sign of her being pulled towards the dance floor.

"This is about as much dancing as I can do", Paige says after catching me watching her, "or a two-step at the most". I watch as she delicately steps from side to side, nodding her head in perfect time to the drumbeat.

"I think you can do better than that". I don't move closer to the dancefloor, but instead, take her hand and twirl her around, swinging our arms wide, letting the melody of the music guide me. We dance like that, stepping side to side, occasionally giving one another a twirl, for song after song after song. A carefree light fills Paige's eyes as her body subconsciously sways to the hypnotic chaos of guitar strings and violins. The frenzy of the music overtakes her shy awkwardness as she submits to the moment and lets go of any lingering worry. As the tempo picks up, she begins to dance anew, her body moving turbulently, all arms and legs; perhaps not a natural dancer, no, but the joy on her face makes her dancing beautiful anyway. I let her pull me into a dance, the feel of her against my body like a welcoming home and I let Paige's joy seep into my own. I let myself live in this moment, granting myself this small opportunity to live like a normal human male, experiencing the tender excitement of falling in love.

Carpe Diem indeed.

Chapter Twenty-Eight

Paige

I don't know what time I ended up stumbling into bed last night, but given how bleary-eyed I feel, I can only guess it was into the early hours of the morning. I stretch, slinging my legs over the side of the bed, only to find my feet land on something warm and squishy, instead of the scratchy feel of the worn carpet. I look down and see Lawrence sprawled on the floor, his chest rising and falling in the steady rhythm of deep sleep. I sit awkwardly, unsure of what to do now. Torn between pulling my legs back onto the bed and pretending to be asleep or continuing my way to the little bathroom, I don't notice Lawrence stir awake beneath my feet.

"Morning", he drawls, his dishevelled hair and sleepy grin causing a swarm of butterflies to erupt in my belly. He makes lying on the floor looking up at me seem like the most natural thing in the world.

"Morning", I reply, bringing my legs underneath me to sit cross-legged at the edge of the bed. "Need a hand up or are you going to continue lying on the floor", I joke and offer him my hand. He grabs hold of it like it's his lifeline to another world, and I give him a little tug until he's crossing his legs beneath him, albeit remaining on the floor rather than joining me on the bed.

"How's your head this morning?", he asks. Up until this point, I was too distracted by his mess of dark hair and charming eyes to notice much else. As if called forth by Lawrence's words, my head pounds insistently, no doubt a consequence of the strong drink from last night and lack of water this morning. I grimace, uncurling my legs to stand up and walk towards the bathroom. Lawrence gives me a knowing look as if he knows the monster his words have unleashed.

"Painful", I choke out as I splash my face with cold water, the icy temperature a shock to my sensitive nerves. Lawrence chuckles from his place on the floor, the sound travelling along the wooden panels of the floor, settling somewhere in the middle of my chest. That sound, the sheer unburdened sibilance of it, nestles in my chest in a way I don't want to examine too closely. I grab a towel from the side, patting my face dry and use the free moisturiser on the side to give life to my tired skin. I turn towards where Lawrence sits on the floor, watching as he gracefully stands up, stretching his arms over his head so that a tiny sliver of skin appears between his trousers and shirt line. I tear my eyes away before he can catch my gawking.

"I better go shower", he nods towards the bedroom door, taking a few steps in that direction. I nod along wordlessly, the glimpse of his torso still reeling through my mind.

"Sure, me too. Shall we meet downstairs in half an hour?", I suggest, finally dragging my eyes up to his own. Lawrence nods in that mysterious way of his, the corner of his mouth tilting up, the dark brown of his eyes light in the early morning sun that peaks through the blinds.

"Sounds good to me". He saunters through the bedroom door, closing it gently on his way out. And I stand watching that closed door longer than I care to admit. The imprint of Lawrence's smile lingers in my mind long after I've jumped into the shower whilst I let the warm water flow luxuriously over my body, the steam of the shower melting my headache away.

Chapter Twenty-Nine

Lawrence

I went to sleep on the floor of her room last night, too content in her presence to leave her for even a few hours. And I fell asleep. Unheard of. I actually slept. Not the half-lucid sleep common to Reapers when we've had a hard day reaping souls, but the restful, unhindered sleep of dreamers, of those hopeful souls who find comfort in the undisturbed hours of unconsciousness.

I get undressed, stepping onto the cold tiles of the shower and let the warm water wash over me. Given the fact I agreed to meet Paige in half an hour, I spend longer than I should soaking in the heat of the water and the crisp scent of body wash provided in every room.

It starts as a tingle at the base of my spine, before becoming a full-scale alarm bell in my head. I rush out of the shower, throwing my clothes on quickly, the peel of bells in my head growing louder by the minute, as I am hauled towards the source of that alarm. The only reason for that beacon of sound, the monstrosity of urgency blaring through my very being, is the signal that someone has died outside of their allotted time. And for a fraction of a second, I am frozen in fear at what this could mean. Because even though it isn't Paige that I'm being pulled towards, for even one soul to die ahead of schedule, means the increased trajectory of everyone else's deaths on my list. It means the increased imminence of Paige's death.

Unable to ignore the sound for a second longer, I let my reaper senses take over, guiding me to the location of the soul awaiting me.

***

A middle-aged man with hair greying at the temples lies semi-recumbent against the wall of a local supermarket. His hand is clutched to his chest, as if trying to push back the source of what killed him. It's a frenzy of panic around him, tears streaming down the face of a comely woman with long, floating brown hair, the hands of a small child clutched tightly between her own. I look inward to the list of souls that hangs perpetually from the walls of my mind. His name is Malcolm Strong, a forty-five-year-old construction worker who was meant to die four months from now in a head-on car crash. Not from a heart attack on a concrete street, surrounded by strangers, being gawked at and pitied like a circus animal.

I crouch down in front of him and close his eyes; any onlookers would just see a soft breeze willing his eyelids down into eternal sleep. It isn't peace that lines his face, in the way that so many humans idealise death, as peaceful, but a blank sort of emptiness. Devoid of anything; no peace, no sadness, just nothing. I search the crowd around him for the tell-tale signs of a soul: blurry edges, frantic eyes, an aura of aching disbelief. Sometimes it takes a while for a soul to show themselves, too busy clinging to their lifeless bodies and the life they're leaving behind, to welcome death with open arms. A chill creeps over my shoulder and I turn towards the pavement to see Malcolm's soul sitting on the curb by the crying woman and little child. I wander over, readying to take his soul into The Beyond.

Seeing me approach, Malcolm turns in my direction, a silent plea on his face as he realises what job I am to carry out.

"Why didn't I have more time?", he beseeches, staring into the face of his little girl, no doubt imagining the future he will no longer get to have with her, the memories and years he no longer gets to enjoy. I don't have words to offer him, the cruelty of the Universe yet again thrown into stark relief. It never gets easier. I say the only thing that I can offer in consolation, a pitiful excuse for comfort if there is any.

"It doesn't make it easier, but be thankful for the time you got", my mind ambles towards Paige whose life will too be cut short, who will live only half the time of the man in front of me. "Some people don't even get that". Malcolm's eyes line with silver as he kneels up to kiss his daughter on the forehead. Then he stands and presses the ghost of a kiss on his wife's lips, his hand hovering over her cheek, a mocking caress of a touch he can no longer give. As if attuned to his very soul, his wife touches her cheek, tracing the phantom touch that Malcolm bestowed, her eyes filled with love and wonder as she feels his presence wrap around her, even in death. With one last look, Malcolm steps away, looking towards me at last, he nods his acceptance.

"We can go now", he says quietly but not weakly, "I've said goodbye".

"Take my hand, you won't feel a thing". And with that, I transport his soul to the shadowed embrace of The Beyond, his life a quiet light that has blinked out, his soul now a thread in the dark tapestry of fate.

I don't linger on the scene to see them take his body away, instead racing back to Paige before she even realises I've been gone.

Chapter Thirty

Lawrence

I check my watch and see that I'm five minutes late to meet Paige. Having brought nothing but what I was already wearing into the room, I hurry out and head downstairs. As I walk into the reception area, I can see Paige sitting on a chair, looking around at the slow trickle of people checking out after staying over.

"Paige", I call, getting her attention. She turns towards me and smiles, the shy kind of smile of someone who isn't quite sure if the events of the night before actually happened.

"Hey, what time do you call this? Thought you'd been washed down the drain", she jokes. She stands up and steps towards me and I can't help but think of kissing her yesterday in that old church. I push that desire down and open the door of the B&B, needing to put some space between us.

"After you", I nod and beckon Paige towards the door. I scan the reception area once more, taking in the homely look of the wooden desk and the worn patterned rugs, unsure if I'll ever come here again. *How can I?* After reaping Paige's soul, I know being near anything that reminds me of her will be too painful. I will fall into the abyss of my job, reaping souls like my lifeless existence depends on it; getting lost in the heady oblivion of soul collecting, to fill the Paige-sized hole that will become my life.

"Do you have much else planned for the day?", Paige asks as we make our long way back to the car. The sky outside is dark for the morning, a herald of the rain soon to come. Without telling her that I need to sort out the mess that is the list of souls I am to collect, I shake my head instead.

"Shall we go over our presentation one last time then before tomorrow?", she asks, peering shyly at me through her hair. All I want is to say yes because as soon as our project is over, I guess it will be time for me to get ready to end her. But then I'm also wary; every extra second I spend with Paige adds another inch to the shape of her in my life. And when she's gone, all those seconds will add up to the hole the lack of her will create.

"Or not...", she trails off, her cheeks going red with embarrassment. She nods her head once, as though affirming something to herself and then strides off ahead of me up the hill, her long legs covering much more distance than I thought her capable of in the space of a few moments. The sight of her walking away from me feels like a dead weight in my stomach. Unable to bear it for a second longer, I run after her. She's now partway down the other side of the hill, her steps uneven as she tries walking quickly downwards which, from my observations of humans, is not an easy feat.

"Paige", I say her name as if it's my own salvation, grabbing her hand and spinning her towards me. Our eyes lock and I can't help but let my gaze travel down to her lips and remember how sweet they tasted against my own. She's so close to me I can feel her heart flutter against my chest; the movement of her throat as she takes a breath, an invitation and a plea. I move my hand to her waist, as I've seen many guys do over the centuries, and use my other hand to tilt her chin up towards me. My hand trembles as I bring my lips down to meet hers, foregoing gentleness as my desire for her takes over. My lips brush against hers, both hands now on her waist as I devour her like a beggar in need of food. Her lips are the cure to my immortality, the taste of her like poison as human desire floods through my veins. My hands move to her back, her hair, her cheeks, greedy in their exploration of her. One touch isn't enough, my skin yearns to know every inch of her. I'm too lost in her to notice as she brings her delicate hands to my chest, pushing me away. I blink in confusion, startled by the new distance between us.

"Lawrence" and fuck if my name doesn't sound like heaven on her lips. She's shaking her head, her mouth trying to form words that won't come out.

I speak before she can continue. "I want to see you later, I just have a few things to sort out first". Like these human feelings I need to get rid of before Anchor finds out and strips me of my title.

"Oh, she says, her shoulders relaxing as the air rushes out of her.

"Oh", I grin and resume walking, taking Paige's hand in mine, indulging myself in her as much as I can. We reach the car too quickly, the seconds passing like missiles through an empty sky and too soon we're driving back to Paige's place and I'm pulling up outside. I turn the engine off and wait for her to undo her seatbelt. She takes her time with the buckle, meticulously placing the belt to the left of the car seat so it won't get stuck in the car door once she's closed it.

"See you later then".

"Yeah, I'll drop round about seven", I say, my eyes locked on the stray piece of hair that's fallen over her forehead. She lingers for a second and then quickly leans in towards me, her mouth brushing mine in farewell, the kiss too quick and sudden before she's stepped out of the car and makes her way towards her front door. I bring my hands to my lips, tracing the ghost of her kiss with my fingers, already excited about seeing her again. But first, I turn the car on and put it in gear, determined to try and sort out the chaos of my list of souls, and hopefully my heart.

Chapter Thirty-One

Lawrence

When I'm in the safety of the four walls of my room at Reaper HQ, I take a seat on the end of my bed and anxiously take out my list of souls. Malcolm was two places ahead of Paige on the list but was also five places down from the next to die. This shouldn't be happening. The fact that it is must mean something big has happened cosmically to shift it out of place.

A knock sounds on my door before I get a chance to look at the list.

"Hey, Law, can I come in?", it's Elodie. I shout yes and the door opens, dim light from the hallway filtering through. "Are you okay? You look... frazzled", she asks, coming to sit on the chair opposite my bed.

"Someone died this morning ahead of his time, like months ahead", I shake my head in confusion and open my palm, the list now pulled forth from the in-between pocket of the Cosmos I usually leave it.

"It's weird but it has been known to happen before".

"I know, it's just never happened to - ", I stop speaking, the air cut from my lunges in shock. I was afraid that I would look at my list of souls and see Paige's name higher up on that list; Malcolm dying early would normally mean all the other names on the list move up position. I'm so surprised by what I see, I can't even finish my sentence.

"Law, what is it?", Elodie asks, now perched on the edge of the seat. She leans forward as though she can read the words on the page before me, but she can't. Each Reaper's list is legible to their eyes only; if Elodie were to show me her list now, it would appear like ink running down a page to me.

"It's Paige. Her name has moved further down my list. She's almost at the bottom".

"What', Elodie looks just as perplexed as I feel. "That can't be right, shouldn't it be the other way around?".

"I don't know. Who are we to question the Universe El? What does your list look like, has anything changed for you? I wonder if something is happening to all Reapers and our charges". Her list appears out of thin air, appearing like magic, a rabbit from a magician's hat. I'm too busy puzzling over my list to be looking at Elodie, but then my ears catch on Elodie's slight intake of breath, a gasp so quiet I can't even be sure I've heard it. I snap my head in her direction. Her forehead is creased with a deep frown, the set of her eyes swimming with confusion, and if I didn't know any better, I would say pain.

"What is it?", I ask in alarm and her features smooth out like marble as though that frown had never been there in the first place. Even though her face now shows no emotion, there's a glimmer of something in her eyes that worries me.

"It's nothing Law, forget about it". I want to push her to tell me, but we've been at this for centuries; I know she'll come to me in her own time, when she's ready. We sit in silence for a few minutes, Elodie staring at the floor until she lets out a big sigh and looks towards me.

"Anyway, I did have a reason for barging into your room", she smiles tentatively at me, and the tension of the past few moments washes away.

"Go on", I say with a sigh, ridding myself of the confusion I feel and tucking it away to puzzle over later when I'm alone.

"I thought we could go to the training room and spar; we haven't trained in a few days".

"Sure, why not. But I have to be done by half six".

"Why, hot date?", Elodie laughs, her laugh a soft twinkle filling the corners of the room. I suppress a wince, her joke erring too close to the truth for comfort. I roll my eyes.

"No, I have a new charge I need to scope out". The fact that I feel the need to lie about spending time with Paige says it all.

"Right", she says, as though not quite believing me. "I'll meet you in the training room in five". She swans out of my room, shutting the door gently behind her. I quickly change my clothes, opting for black joggers and a plain black sports shirt, and head down to train.

***

Even though Reapers encompass the promise of peace in death and so have little need for violence, we need to know basic self-defence and offensive moves for times when we encounter vengeful or restless spirits, who continue to fight the idea of death even after they have already succumbed to it.

We've been training for half an hour now, going through the different techniques needed to subdue an angry spirit. They're quick little things that can move faster than light, their fear great motivators to evade capture. As soon as we're able to touch one, the hard part is done and they pass through our bodies into The Beyond. It's capturing them that can prove difficult.

"Your go", Elodie wheezes, pointing towards the sprint track she's just finished running. "You got this", she winks, taking a seated position on the floor, she starts stretching her legs out.

I take a slow jog for the first stretch of the track, making sure to warm my muscles up. And even though I know this is training and shouldn't be enjoyed, the feel of the air moving past me and the fluidity of my muscles as I run has always been the closest taste of freedom I've ever had. My feet pick up speed as I fly across the running track; the barest touch of my feet down on the gravel floor; the power of my body as I move so fast: it is everything. The only other time I've felt this kind of rush is when I kiss Paige. And that is forbidden. I take a lap around the course a few times, trying to increase my speed with each circuit, chasing imaginary ghosts in front of me, and leaving my confusing feelings in the dust behind me.

"Nice work", Elodie says from the floor, "I haven't seen you go that fast in a while" she acknowledges.

"Thanks, pushing myself felt good today", *I needed it*, I don't add. I offer her a hand up and pull her to her feet. "Shall we do ten minutes of combat and then call it a day?", I walk over to the mats not waiting for her answer. I walk the two of us through a series of manoeuvres, flowing from one position to the next. My body takes over, moving into the next position without much thought, the ease of practice and muscle memory taking over. It's a cross between what humans call yoga and then self-defence; postures that help with balance and stability as well as movements that protect our bodies from malevolent spirits.

"Thanks for letting me tag along", I tell Elodie once we've finished combat and are tidying up.

"Anytime, it's mandatory anyway but it feels like we haven't caught up since we last went to the pyramids". She looks at me as if recalling our previous conversation and my stomach turns over. I hope she doesn't ask about Paige because I know the second she does, I'll confess everything to her and I wouldn't be able to stand the disappointment. "How are you doing?", she asks. How can I tell her it feels like I'm dying inside, that part of me can't breathe with the weight of Paige's death hovering over me.

"I'm - " I open my mouth, trying to think of what to say but I don't want to lie to my best friend. "Sometimes this life is hard, harder than I imagined it would be". Elodie looks at me as if she gets it, something in her gaze giving me the confidence to continue. "I don't know what makes Paige different, El, but I find myself needing to know her. When it comes to her, it isn't just work, it's my life".

"Law, you don't have a life. And I'm not saying that to be mean, I just want you to be careful. It might seem fun and endearing now but it will only cause more pain in the end. More than you know". She swallows, "You're playing a dangerous game, a game you're going to lose".

"I'm not playing any games...", I trail off, the lie tasting sour in my mouth. Elodie doesn't reply, the look on her face is answer enough.

"I best go shower and change before Reaper duties continue". I give her a nod farewell and walk out of the training room. I chance a glance back over my shoulder. Elodie stands in the centre of the room, her list of souls in her hand. As if sensing my attention her head kicks up. Her eyes are lined with silver and the look she gives me fills me with such anxiety and worry that I need to know what's bothering her. I turn around and go to take a step towards her, but Elodie just shakes her head. I stay standing where I am, watching my best friend wrestle with something I can't even guess at, and watch as she lets herself disappear, spiriting away to who knows where.

I don't linger in the training room and head straight back to my room, but the look on Elodie's face follows my every step, her face on my mind as I shower and get changed. Even the thought of an evening with Paige isn't quite sweet enough to completely erase that look in her eye or the uneasy feeling that now sits like a rock in my stomach.

Chapter Thirty-Two

Paige

Lawrence said he'd come around about seven, so I have a few hours to myself before I need to start getting ready. Feeling too tired to read, I decide to make a coffee and watch some tv. Opting for something a bit different, I add some hot chocolate powder to the bottom of my glass to make a mocha. Coffee in hand, I take a seat on my two-seater sofa, grabbing the tv remote and turning the telly on. Although reading with a good book in bed is the height of comfort, there is something to be said about snuggling down in front of the telly, mindlessly losing yourself for hours in the lights and flare of modern-day television. The series I'm currently getting lost in is Charmed; a programme about three sisters who discover that they're witches and have to battle demons and the Source of all Evil on a daily basis. Even though I've watched Charmed more times than I can count, watching the scenes and plot twists play out never gets old to me. If anything, I enjoy watching it again to see what new things I'll notice this time round, or if I pick up on any anachronisms within the plot, where the creators have made an error in the story or cast an actor in two different roles, expecting us not to notice.

I spend the next hour or so watching Phoebe break apart over Cole's betrayal, her heart torn in two over the revelation of Cole's real identity. And even though I can't begin to imagine what true heartbreak feels like, or the pain of loving someone who is ultimately bad for you, I've always envied the love Cole and Phoebe share. Cole's love for Phoebe is so pure that he overcomes being evil for her, even if it's short-lived. Being loved to that extreme is every little girl's fantasy; knowing that someone chose you no matter what, would die and claw their way back from hell just to keep their love for you alive, is the kind of passion one could only dream of. I'd be lying if I said that I didn't one day hope to feel even a fraction of what Phoebe and Cole feel for each other with someone else if I'm so lucky.

My phone pings, bringing me back to the real world. It's Lawrence, saying he'll be round in about half an hour. Heartbroken and remade within the space of a few episodes, I let time get away from me, now feeling as though I'll have to rush to get ready. Switching off the tv, I grab my mug and swill it in the sink, then head upstairs for a quick shower. I decide to make more of an effort this evening, opting for a casual, navy blue floaty dress. If this is the last time I see Lawrence outside of uni, since our project will be presented tomorrow, I at least want to leave a lasting impression. Not used to wearing dresses all that often, I feel a bit awkward and uncomfortable. But I refuse to let that bother me too much, pushing myself out of my comfort zone is how I get used to these things. I've just finished adding a few curls to my hair when I hear the doorbell ring. Checking my watch, I see that Lawrence has arrived at seven on the dot. There's nothing more attractive than a man on time. I smile to myself as I walk down the stairs, eyes flitting around frantically to check no dishes need washing or rubbish needs putting away. Everything is kept nice and tidy, being as I'm a neat freak, but you can never be too sure.

"Hey", I greet Lawrence as I open the door and it's clear I'm not the only one trying to make an effort tonight. Although he still has on his usual black t-shirt and jeans, his hair is gelled back from his face, highlighting his strong jawline and depthless eyes. Just that slight change of having his hair pushed back makes such a difference: rather than the brooding, mysterious Lawrence I've come to expect, he seems open, almost nervous.

"You look", he pauses, staring at me as though seeing me for the first time. "You look beautiful Paige". The sound of my name on his tongue is like a prayer, one I'd give anything to hear repeated over and over again.

"Thank you", I blush "you look good too Lawrence". Surprise lights his eyes as though he wasn't expecting the compliment. He smiles down at me, gratitude in his eyes as I usher him inside.

"I left our project notes upstairs with my laptop, so just make yourself comfortable whilst I go grab them". Lawrence nods and that's all the confirmation I need before dashing upstairs and back down again in a few minutes flat.

"You have a nice place, I like how many books you have", Lawrence says, having made his way towards the far wall of the living room that houses all my books. His hand trails a path over different covers, randomly picking titles to skim before making their way to new unventured pages.

"Do you read?", I ask as I make my way towards him.

"No, in all my years, I can count on my hand the number of books I've read, but the idea of reading has always fascinated me". The way he talks makes it seem as though he's lived thousands of years, but it must just be a figure of speech.

"In all your years? If I didn't know any better, I'd say you're suggesting that you've lived for centuries", I laugh. "But you're young, now could be the time you start reading, think of all the years you still have ahead of you". He looks over at me before replying, a spark of something old behind his eyes.

"This world of ours ages us before we're ready. I feel as though I've lived a thousand minutes but none of them made sense to me, none of them had meaning until recently". Breaking eye contact, he turns back to the bookshelf before I respond, his fingers a continuous wave over broken and well-read spines. His hand hovers over one of my favourite books, *Looking for Alaska,* the blue spine so worn, every time I open it, the book automatically opens to somewhere in the middle.

"You can borrow that book if you like. It's relatively short so would be a nice first book. It's also one of my favourites. Something about the ending just sticks with me. Each time I pick it up, it reminds me to be grateful for my gift of life and my time exploring the labyrinth. It's hard not to like it". I smile at him. I step towards the shelf, my hand moving over his as I pull the book out.

"Exploring the labyrinth?", he asks quizzically as I hand him the book. His hand closes around the book, the pads of his fingers skimming my palm, sending a rush of pleasure through me. Just that small contact is enough to cause butterflies to take flight through my nervous system.

"It will make sense once you read the book, promise". He nods, a small smile appearing at the corner of his mouth.

"I hope it does, otherwise I'll be demanding a refund".

"You can't have a refund on something you haven't actually bought", I quip back. He stands there thoughtfully, and I'm about to announce my verbal victory.

"If not a refund, then some other form of payment". I can't tell if he's flirting or just making a joke, but I feel flustered all the same.

"Luckily, I know it will make sense, so no payment will be needed", although if by payment, he meant a kiss, I'm secretly hoping that he doesn't get the reference. And by the look in his eye, longing mixed with something else, I can't help but wonder if he also hopes the same thing.

"So, the project", I change the subject, moving over to the small wooden table in my kitchen area, desperate to move away from my romantic fantasies. "I thought we could go over what each of us would say and then see if it's worth adding any detail before submitting it through the online portal". Lawrence takes a seat across from the one I stand behind, waiting expectantly for me to open my laptop. "I doubt it will take too long, it's mostly finished anyway...", I leave my sentence unfinished. I hope it takes longer than I think, since I sort of wanted to spend the whole evening with Lawrence, getting to know him more, before the inevitable demise of our friendship? Fling? Companionship? Tomorrow once the presentation has finished.

"If it doesn't take too long, we can always just hang out afterwards, I have nothing else planned this evening". My heart gives a little squeeze as he gives words to the thoughts in my head. But the insecure little voice on my shoulder questions whether he actually wants to spend time with me or if his saying he has no other plans just equates to him having nothing better to do. Shutting down that insidious whisper, I pull out a chair and sit down. I open my laptop, the presentation already open as I have a habit of not closing my tabs down. My argument is that it saves time when I log back on to start work; rather than having to faff about finding where everything is stored, it's ready and waiting for me.

We spend the next hour adding to our presentation, giving our victim Toby more hobbies and interests, as though creating this fictional life he had will somehow give him more meaning behind the heart attack we're meant to be writing about. Lawrence decides that he wants to be the one to present Toby's life before his untimely death, leaving me to cover the symptoms, causes, and the final diagnosis of what our victim suffered from. As we discuss things that Toby could have enjoyed, like skiing or wild horse riding and all other extreme and completely unlikely hobbies, it's like watching Lawrence come alive. He takes such an interest in the extreme sports that he grabs my laptop from me and types them into Google so he can watch videos of people doing it in real life. We talk about food and what Toby's favourite cuisine could be. Like my own, I think it should be Chinese, because who doesn't enjoy tasty rice and curry sauce every few weeks?

"I have to admit, I've never had Chinese before, so I can't comment", Lawrence says, his head down, adding Chinese to Toby's personality list. I'm too surprised to know what to say at first. But then I laugh and grab my phone.

"Well, that's about to change. I can't allow that to continue", I smile at Lawrence. I ring my local Chinese, ordering a few different dishes so Lawrence can experience a wide range of the menu. "Ordered", I put the phone down and face Lawrence.

"They said it would take around half an hour which should give us time to finish up and submit the presentation".

"You didn't have to do that'" he says, looking almost embarrassed.

"Why wouldn't I? I'm getting hungry anyway so would need food at some point. I'm also intrigued to watch you experience Chinese food for the first time", I grin as a hint of a blush paints his cheeks.

"Hopefully I enjoy it as much as Toby", he winks at me. The next ten minutes fly by. With the last touches of our presentation complete, we submit it with a collective sigh.

"Feels good to have that finished, doesn't it?", I ask, the satisfying relief of getting something finished before a deadline washing over me.

"It does feel good; it feels good to finish something". Lawrence smiles at me and helps me pack my laptop and other messes away.

"Shall we put the telly on whilst we wait for the food to arrive?", I ask. Now that work is out the way, Charmed beckons me, the addictive romance and battle of good vs evil pulling me towards the sofa. "I've been watching Charmed, but we can put something else on if you'd prefer?".

"Charmed? What is it about?".

Cringing I explain the main premise of the programme, hoping he doesn't think me too immature for my proclivity towards fantasy and the supernatural.

"Sounds interesting". Lawrence takes a seat on my sofa. He

makes himself comfortable, putting his arm along the back of the cushion, stretching his legs out in front of him. Taking that as confirmation, I turn the tv on and resume watching Charmed, sinking next to Lawrence on the sofa, the presence of his company and the familiarity of Charmed wrapping me in contented comfort. We sit in comfortable silence until the doorbell rings, heralding the arrival of our food.

Chapter Thirty-Three

Paige

I pay for the Chinese and Lawrence comes up behind me, taking the box of yummy food out of my hands and carrying it over to the kitchen. He unpacks the tin foil cartons with meticulous efficiency, lining them up along the kitchen counter like military soldiers standing in battle formation. I reach up over his right shoulder, grabbing two plates down from the cupboard. My hand brushes his shoulder and I hear his slight intake of breath at the small contact. I put the plates on the side, scooping a bit of food from each carton onto our plates so we've both got a mix of a few different things. Before putting some chips on our plates, I take the lid off the curry sauce, dipping my chip into the warm, salty liquid. I take a bite, resisting the urge to sigh at the heavenly taste. I can see Lawrence looking at me from the corner of his eye, a small smile tugging at his lips.

"Here, try it", I pass him a curry-dipped chip. "The best part of a Chinese is the obligatory curry sauce dip at the start. Trust me", I laugh. Lawrence tentatively brings the chip to his lips, scepticism clear on his face. The scepticism is quickly replaced with a grin as he takes another chip and puts it in his mouth.

"If the rest of the Chinese tastes this good, I can see why it would be Toby's favourite food".

"I knew you'd like it". I hand him his plate and we make our way back over to the sofa. We continue watching Charmed as we eat but I can't help sneaking glances at Lawrence to watch his reaction to the food. With each bite of food he takes, he seems to settle into himself, and I let the peace he exudes wash over me. Once we've both finished eating, we put our empty plates on the coffee table. Lawrence puts his arm over the back of the sofa, moving closer to me, his knee brushing mine where they're curled up underneath me. He interrupts every now and then asking who the characters are as he tries to follow the plot. The episode we're watching is called 'Death takes a Halliwell'. When I was younger, it wasn't one that piqued my interest because the plot for the episode is rather tame, lacking the onscreen action of magical powers and scary demons. As I've gotten older and watched it again, the real meaning and nuisances of the episode have been brought forth for me. As the episode closes with Prue speaking to the Angel of Death, Lawrence turns towards me, a question brimming on the tip of his tongue.

"Does Prue die later in the season?", he asks, and the question throws me a little, considering he's never watched nor heard of Charmed before tonight.

"Why would you ask that?", I answer his question with a question, curious to see what prompted him to guess the plot twist at the end of season three.

"It's obvious, isn't it? I mean, the only reason that Prue can still see Death at the end of the episode is because she's still on his list", he pauses, clearly working through the plot in his head. "The whole point of the episode isn't even about saving the innocent or not. It's about making death familiar to both Prue and her sisters. If they don't see him as an enemy, how can they hate what they will soon come to lose? They will be broken by her loss, but also accepting of it, knowing that the will of the Universe always wins out over human connection". Even though he speaks with confidence, he seems undeniably sad. The end-credit music plays in the background as Lawrence edges closer to me, his eyes never leaving mine.

"Yeah, she does die", I answer his original question. "But I think the notion of getting to know Death, in the effort of making it easier, is a load of nonsense. It's never easy; it's too final. People might lie and say grief gets easier with time, and I guess I'm lucky enough to not have had the experience of that yet, but I know in my heart that those words are just comfort. All death does is make us realise how precious our lives are. I will always rebel against the idea of death because I want to make sure I've lived all that I can before I'm stricken down, you know?", I say. And I guess it's true; even if it is someone's time, the idea of death is never an easy one. Even if I spend most of my time living between the pages of my books, the crippling loss of fictional characters has taught me that.

"Yes", Lawrence whispers and it sounds like an answer to a question I never even asked. "Yes Paige, that's it". As if realising something I'm not privy to, he leans across the distance between us, brushing my cheek with his thumb. A gesture so sincere and gentle that uneasy warmth spreads through me. I could get used to these touches of affection. I open my mouth to ask what he's agreeing to but don't get the chance. Instead, his mouth is on mine and the feverish touch of his lips is the opposite to the gentle caress of his hand on my cheek. There's a yearning and a hunger in his kiss and I get lost in it. My hands find their way to his neck of their own accord; my knees knocking against his thighs in a bid to get closer to him. He breaks away for air and sighs my name.

"Paige, Paige, Paige", the more he says it, the more I want to pull him back to me and feel my name whispered against my lips. I want to drink his words into my being, as though I can capture this moment on my skin. There's nothing better than the feeling of my body acting on pure instinct; no thoughts, just action. And that kind of abandon is so freeing. But like always, the heady rush of happiness is soon squandered by reality, making moments of pure feeling fleeting. Lawrence pulls away and moves away from me on the sofa. The absence of his body is like a physical blow, leaving me cold and uncertain in his presence.

"I should go Paige. I'll see you tomorrow for the presentation".

"Lawrence, wait', I follow him to the door, trying to figure out what to say to make the whole situation less sad and uncomfortable. "It was just a kiss, it doesn't have to mean anything".

"But you don't understand Paige, it means *everything*. It is everything". The anguish in his voice gives me pause.

"I don't - " I begin to say, but he cuts me off.

"You wouldn't get it and I don't expect you to. The last few weeks with you have been so good Paige. Thank you". He nods and opens the door. But why does it sound like he's saying goodbye? I don't understand.

"See you tomorrow". He leans in one last time and presses a gentle kiss on my forehead before walking out the door and closing it behind him.

***

Lawrence doesn't show up for the presentation, so I'm forced to present it on my own, and I can't help but feel as though yesterday was the last time I'll see him.

Chapter Thirty-Four

Lawrence

It's the second time in all of my existence that I fall asleep. For a species that doesn't sleep, it's hard to shake this ominous feeling that something is happening to me. After leaving Paige's last night, I came straight to my room at Reaper HQ, a trembling mess of energy. Lying down on the bed, I closed my eyes, hoping the absence of sight would help calm my nerves. Instead, I woke up five hours later, Paige's name a sweet caress on my lips. I can still taste her on my lips despite having slept and many hours passing. I've fallen in deeper than I ever should have allowed myself; perhaps Anchor was right and I'm not fit for the job.

And it wasn't just the taste of Paige or her smile or her company that tipped me past a point of no return. The whole evening last night was like putting both feet into the human world for the first time; leaving behind this empty existence and masquerading as one of them. I've never needed to eat before, but I can see why humans do. It was slightly horrifying yet decadently satisfying how good the food tasted to me. What would normally taste like ash on my tongue, suddenly had flavour. Again, anxiety over these changes floods my system. But it's all secondary to *that* feeling. That feeling of just sitting and being at one with Paige whilst the tv was on, was the kind of peace I've never even known before. But the irony of what we watched wasn't lost on me. My duty seems to be lurking behind every corner, Prue's run-in with Death a Cosmic mirror to Paige's own fate. And it's another reminder that I can't afford to ignore. I have to create some distance now, otherwise I know I won't be able to carry out my job. With my newfound resolution, I jump in the shower and get dressed, heading off to give the presentation with Paige, the last thing we'll do together before her time comes to an end.

***

Students crowd outside the seminar room, chatting about what they got up to the previous evening and how they found the assignment. Paige stands to the side of the door that leads into the room, her gaze fixed on her phone, her eyes darting back and forth across the screen as though she's engrossed in something. She looks up every now and again, scanning the hall of students for something, someone. I can only guess that the person she's looking for is me. The doors leading into the hall open and her head whips around and it's the hope in her eyes, something that goes far beyond the mere hope of not having to present the project solo, that gives me pause. And it's then that I realise I can't go through with the presentation, because speaking to her, seeing her smile at me as we joke about our poor victim, will crumble my resolve in ten seconds flat.

I let myself disappear before she sees me, existing in the in-between folds between earth and the Universe. To everybody in the hall, it just looks like the doors opened on a phantom wind. As I push the doors closed, the light in Paige's eyes dims just a little and I watch as she turns back towards the classroom, rolling her eyes slightly; at what, I'm not sure. The tutor opens the door and beckons the students in, Paige taking her time to file in behind her classmates. I can see the inner battle waging within her, her tense shoulders and stiff legs, fighting the urge to look around once more, to look for me one more time.

I can feel something in my chest delicately breaking. Is this what humans describe as heartache? Is this what it means to love? But as Paige walks away from me, and into the classroom, I can't help but feel as though she's taking something of myself with her. I don't stay and watch her present, needing to let her live the next few weeks without me. Needing to live my next few weeks without her. Needing this space so I can do the job I've been ordained to do by the Universe. And as I fade away into the nothingness of the Cosmos, my cheeks start to dampen with the beginnings of goodbye.

Chapter Thirty-Five

Paige

Mine and Lawrence's names were called second, so I'm one of the first to present. I don't really remember much, other than trying to frantically power through the presentation without my nerves getting the best of me. Once the ordeal of presenting is over, I can sit and listen to my classmates' presentations in relative comfort. All the presentations are fairly good, and it's been interesting to see everyone's individual takes on the assignment.

Once Thom dismisses us, telling us we'll get our grades over the next few weeks, I stand, packing my things into my rucksack. Heidi holds the door open for me as I head out of the classroom and I take the time to tell her how good I thought her presentation was.

"Really", she beams, "thank you!".

"Yeah, it was really good and you didn't even seem nervous at all whilst presenting", I laugh, knowing I probably looked like a tomato under the glare of all my peers whilst I presented alone. *Because Lawrence didn't come.* I push the thought aside, not wanting to linger on the pain fluttering through my chest at his lack of appearance.

"What happened to your partner", Heidi asks, as if the Universe sensed turmoil and wanted to make it worse.

"He's ill", I say, the lie rolling off my tongue.

"Too bad. You did well by yourself though, you should be proud", she smiles at me as we walk out of the building.

"Thank you", I blush, never one to receive compliments well.

"Have you got another class now?" Heidi asks.

"No, I was just going to go to the library and do the reading for next week's lectures".

"Oh nice, mind if I join?"

"Not at all". We make our way to the library building, Heidi chatting about what she got up to at the weekend and the other seminar classes she's got for the week. I take this small moment of socialisation as a little win and give myself an imaginary pat on the back. She asks what I did at the weekend and I tell her about my job lifeguarding and the current book I'm reading. I omit hanging out with Lawrence for multiple reasons. One, because the time we spent together feels intimate, and sharing it with anyone would be like unwrapping a bow, that falls flat and crumbles under closer scrutiny and no matter how I might try and retie it, it would never quite look as it once did. And secondly, because Lawrence's absence today has left me hollow; I'm unlikely to see him again now so why torture myself by running over the events of our time together?

"No way", she exclaims "We're reading that book at the moment in my book club. You should join our next meeting!".

"Really?", I say, both pleased to be asked but also apprehensive.

"Yes definitely", she grins.

We grab a table just inside the entrance to the library and spend the hour or so I had planned on reading chatting about different books and holidays Heidi plans on taking next summer instead. Heidi talks at a hundred miles a minute, flipping from one topic to the next without even taking a breath. It's almost hard to keep up.

"There's this organisation that arranges group trips abroad for students which I've signed up to", Heidi tells me and I find myself intrigued. Travelling with a group of students could be cool, at least it beats travelling alone, not that I would know what either feels like.

"That sounds amazing, what's the group called?", I ask.

"I can't remember off the top of my head" she laughs, "but give me your number and I'll text it to you when I get back to my flat. I have a leaflet somewhere in the mess of my room". I do just that, keying my phone number into her phone.

"Perfect, thank you", I grin.

"I've got another lecture now", Heidi says after checking her watch "Apologies for the lack of studying we did".

"Don't worry at all, this was much more enjoyable", I laugh as we both stand up and make our way out of the library.

"I'll text you the details of the travel group and the next book club meeting".

"Can't wait", and I really can't. I'm *excited* at the prospect of meeting new people, which is a complete first for me.

"See you soon", Heidi waves, turning right towards the science building where I turn left to head to my car. It isn't until I'm in my driving home that Lawrence pops into my head, my earlier disappointment hitting me like a physical blow. I try not to dwell on it because feeling sad over something I can't change will only make me feel worse.

Chapter Thirty-Six

Paige

Despite going back to a relatively uneventful life now that Lawrence has ceased to make an appearance, I can't lie and say I didn't take something away from our time together. Refusing to be a recluse, and spending all my free time inside, I've made an effort to get out more, either by myself or with other people. I wished I'd lived this way sooner. Heidi texted me not long after I made it home, telling me book club is next week and I'm looking forward to delving into the different theories people have about how the third book in the Empyrean series by Rebecca Yarros will play out. I've been spending time with Ari, Lillith and Brando outside of work. I've found that once I made an effort to get to know them, we had more in common than I originally thought. The four of us are in the middle of rock climbing at one of the local warehouses when Ari pulls me to the side so it's just the two of us.

"Enjoying yourself?", he asks.

"Yeah", I nod, "but it's definitely harder than it looks! Not that you seem to be struggling all that much", I laugh. Ari is built like a machine, the muscles of his biceps straining against the tight sleeves of his white t-shirt. I would almost accuse him of picking this activity as an excuse to flex his well-earned muscles, but he isn't like that; he's quite humble when it comes to his appearance. When looking at him, with his tight tops, big muscles, and well-groomed blond hair, you might assume he's a bit arrogant and self-centred, but he's really quite down to earth.

He's nice. Dare I say too nice sometimes.

"You'll get the hang of it, it just takes practice". I nod along, knowing he's right. Being able to master rock climbing will be something I need to commit myself to. But I've enjoyed the way my muscles strain as I try and pull myself higher. Just another thing I've learnt I like whilst pushing myself out of my comfort zone. And again, even knowing how things played out, I can only find myself thanking Lawrence for it. I shake my head, banishing thoughts of him from my mind.

"I'm sure I will", I agree.

"Paige", Ari pauses as though steeling himself for something. Despite my desire to banish Lawrence from my mind, I can't help but think about how the way Ari says my name lacks the cadence with which it fell from Lawrence's lips. "I've enjoyed the last few weeks getting to know you more. I wondered if you'd maybe be interested in doing something one-on-one, just the two of us", he asks. I take a moment or two to answer, trying to decide if I even feel remotely attracted to him. I think he's nice and I can see how other people would find him good looking. *But do I? I'm not sure.* His cheeks start to redden the longer his words float between us unanswered.

"It's nice of you to ask", I begin, with every intention of saying no. But isn't part of living taking risks with your heart, allowing people to crawl between the walls you put up, creating a them-shaped space in your life? Not all romance has to be flying sparks, a heady rush of feeling when you look at them, a fire in your veins at the slightest touch. I read somewhere that love is meant to be safe; it isn't meant to be explosive and dramatic, causing imbalances and constant fluctuations of emotions. And I guess that's what Ari could be, a stable romance? One where I feel secure. Even if it amounts to nothing, I guess going on one date couldn't harm. "I would really like that".

"Really?", he beams, as though he expected me to say no.

"Yeah", I nod, a small smile making its way across my face at the excitement that radiates from Ari. I guess it feels nice that someone seems so excited to spend time with me. And who knows? Maybe it will be nice, maybe I'll surprise myself and actually have a good time. I can see Brando and Lilith making their way over to us. Brando wipes his chalk-stained hands over Lilith's purple jumper and she shrieks in mock outrage.

"I'll text you later about it", Ari says quickly, his cheeks turning red again.

"Text her about what?" Lilith enquires, nothing if not nosey. Ari sputters, opening his mouth to speak but no words come out.

"Just about hanging out", I supply, giving Ari a curious look. Is he embarrassed to say he asked me out? Or does he just not want to make a big deal out of it in case it doesn't go well? I guess it could be awkward for our group dynamic if the date goes up in flames.

"Nice", Brando jumps in, "I do so love our little group activities", he winks at me and his boyish charm eases the awkward tension. Ari shakes his head, having some kind of internal war with himself. The battle lost, Ari looks at me, smiling apologetically, and the four of us make plans for next week to go to the cinemas. We all walk out together and head to our own cars.

"I'll text you", Ari promises, as he walks past me, heading down the road to the bus stop. Ari doesn't drive, and whilst in the past I've considered this a bit of a red flag, I'm trying to be open-minded about it and not so critical. We haven't even arranged a date yet, so I need to stop obsessing over such small details. As I sit in my car, I lean my head against the steering wheel, wishing for my brain to slow down and not overthink every little thing. It's exhausting.

As I reverse out of the car park, I put my music on, banging my head and singing along like I'm an honorary member of the band. I would never sing in public, but those moments when I'm alone and no one is watching? I perform like I was born to be on stage. Nothing beats that rush of screaming until your lungs give out and committing yourself to living so completely in the moment of that one song. That's what I like so much about it: you can lose yourself in it until nothing exists but the melody.

Chapter Thirty-Seven

Paige

The drive back from rock climbing flew by, my music obnoxiously loud as I drove with my windows down to let some air in, my body still warm from the exertion of exercise. Wanting to wash the chalk and sweat of today's climb off my skin, I jump in the shower. I keep the shower water on scalding, just the way I like it, a habit I stick to even in the thick of summer. No amount of good weather will ever be able to justify a cold shower. Ever.

After luxuriating in the hot water for a good half an hour, letting the water wash over me in a relaxing monsoon, I hear my phone go off as I wrap my towel around me. As promised, Ari has texted me, following up on plans. He asks if I'm free tonight to go for a drink. I had planned on treating myself to a night in with a good book, since I've just finished all my uni work for this semester. I've now picked up extra shifts at work to try and fill the long hours of the winter holidays, noticeably longer if you're a uni student, so the fact that I'm working early tomorrow is also another reason not to go. *Or I guess being in work tomorrow could be a reason to leave early if I'm not having a good time.* Smiling to myself at my mischievous little plan, I text Ari back and we arrange where we'll meet. We said we'd meet at six at a bar not too far from where we rock climbed this morning. I've never been myself but Lilith raves about it constantly; a frequent haunt of hers whenever she's out looking for some fun.

With it being just a little after twelve, I decide I can still give myself an indulgent hour or two of reading before doing a few chores and getting ready. Having recently finished *Iron Flame*, a six-hundred-plus tome by Rebecca Yarros, I gave myself a few days off reading to allow for the obligatory book hangover that comes after finishing hefty fantasy book. The male characters are so delicious and addictive that it's hard not to get withdrawals from the sizzling romance and epic world-building found in the novel. I've re-read the book multiple times, and each time I fall in love with them that little bit more.

I walk over to my bookshelf, letting my eyes wander over the many read titles and those I've never picked up. I have a rather small to-be-read stack at the end of the bottom shelf, a sign that a trip to the bookshop is much needed. I trail my hands over the spines, much like Lawrence did, trying to decide what I'm in the mood for. My hand pauses over the space where *Looking for Alaska* should be. After Lawrence not turning up for our presentation, my heart sinks a little at the thought that I may never get that book back. A book I've read so many times it's a kaleidoscope of highlights, each time I read it I find new meaning in different lines. Pushing the pang in my chest aside, the loss of never seeing that book again not the only loss that's on my mind, I settle on reading *Wuthering Heights*. I've only read it once and it was quite difficult to get through; the narration all over the place, the plot, at times hard to follow. But I'm a sucker for a good romance and the one between Catherine and Heathcliff is more tragic than that of Romeo and Juliet. Despite only having read it once, I have multiple copies of the book. Although I don't buy into the romantic pedestal that publishers put on the classics because of their marketing skills when it comes to the beautiful book covers they seem to endlessly churn out, the classics are best sellers. It's the art of *selling* the book that makes writers famous, not necessarily the contents within. This copy of the novel is pale pink, a gothic-style drawing of Catherine on the front. It's almost a caricature, the features of Catherine's face over exaggerated and unsymmetrical. It's intriguing.

I place the book on my sofa, going to grab a coffee to drink whilst I snuggle down, ready to travel back to Victorian England. I don't even feel as though I need a coffee, it's more habitual at this point; I can't even think about reading in the middle of the day without an obligatory coffee to accompany it. Coffee made and on the table beside me, I pick up the novel and start reading…

I let time wash away as Emily Bronte whisks me towards the woes and isolation of the troubled Heathcliff.

Chapter Thirty-Eight

Lawrence

I always secretly laughed at the humans who seemed unable to possess even an ounce of self-control; weak nobodies with no backbone who profess self-control to be the enemy, when in fact, their lack of motivation has always seemed to me to be the root of their disease.

But now I get it, fuck have I ever.

The last few weeks have been a serious lesson in self-control. I've thrown myself into reaping souls, watching my list as Paige's name gets further away, to distract my one-track mind from thoughts of Paige. I may have checked on Paige once or twice from a distance and she seems happy. She's been hanging out with people she never mentioned, and I can't help the ugly curl of jealousy that sits like a new organ in my stomach when I happen to see some blond-haired, over-muscled guy stare at her longingly when she's not paying attention. Just the thought of her with someone else steals my breath. And this angry jealousy is so new to me, I'm too caught up in this torment to feel relief that she's out living her life, just like I wanted her to. Except without me.

But tonight is the first time in a few weeks that I haven't been rushed off my feet. I planned on asking Elodie if she wanted to go the Pyramids, or if she wanted help with any of her wayward souls, but I couldn't find her – I can't help but get the feeling that she's avoiding me. Sat in my room, the book Paige lent me stares at me accusingly; thrown on my side table, I haven't looked at it since the night she lent it to me all those weeks ago. *Looking for Alaska.* There's something about the name of it that draws you in; I wonder if it's an adventure novel since Alaska is somewhere in America. Could it be about discovering new lands? Resisting the urge to peek on Paige again, I decide now is as good a time as any to jump into this so-called labyrinth that Paige mentioned. The intrigue at such a strange comment comes back two-fold from when Paige first mentioned it. I take a seat in the chair by my dresser and flick through the pages. Different pages are dogged-eared and there are many highlighted sections, sometimes in yellow, sometimes pink, and sometimes even orange. I wonder what each of these lines means to Paige, for surely that is the point of the highlighting, to spotlight the parts that have significance to her, that resonate with her soul? The book intrigues me even more now – not only will I be reading the story, but I'll also be reading Paige's experience of it. And how intimate it will be for me to learn what her soul feels, hidden between the pages of this book.

I turn to the first page and it only has one word on it:

Before.

Wanting to know what and who this before refers to, I read on, the life of Miles Halter and his start at Culver Creek surprisingly endearing.

***

Forty pages in and I begin to embark on this journey of the labyrinth. Paige has highlighted a particularly lengthy section, that seems to settle in the hollow parts of me and create space. It talks of what it means to be a living person, how intricate and impossible the physical practice of being alive truly is. And fuck if those words don't give a voice to that whisper in my mind I've tried to ignore since I first looked into Paige's blue eyes. *What is the meaning behind life?* I ask myself as I carry on reading.

As I read on, that question echoes round in mind.

Humanity comes alive for me between the two hundred and sixty two pages of the book. I feel like I'm living through my many 'firsts', navigated through Mile's life. Before college, he seemed to have little to no friends, and now he has a whole group of them. And so it is that I too have made friends, friends with these different personalities, penned in black and white. The attraction Miles feels for Alaska? I feel it too, albeit differently. Everything about her that intrigues him has parallels between myself and Paige. The curve of her lips and the secret smile hidden away along its edges. The way her hair falls with little effort down her back. There is but one stark difference between Alaska and Paige, and that's confidence. Where Alaska is bold and daring, Paige is quiet, reserved. But I can almost hear Paige's longing to be different, to come out of her own shell. Her highlights shout out to me how she wants to leave her mark on this earth before her time here is over.

And don't all humans want something like that? I even find myself with that same longing, despite existing on a different plane to humanity. I want to leave a mark behind. I used to think that I would find peace, slowly dissolving into nothing, when the call of the Reaper no longer rang out to me. But now this nothingness is exactly what I fear. The yearning I've felt towards Paige over the last few weeks of knowing her has evolved into a yearning for life. *To be something more.* The more I read and experience living through Miles' eyes, the more I realise that I cannot put these feelings back; the proverbial genie is out of the bottle and there is nothing to be done for it.

I devour each page like a man long deprived of food, so engrossed in the words that I'm halfway through before I realise it. Halfway through when tragedy strikes, and I am again reminded of the fragility of human life. A quick glance at the clock besides me says it's almost nine in the morning, meaning I've been reading for over nine hours. And yet I cannot get enough. Needing to know how Miles will now cope in his Alaska-less world, hoping to find some courage for me to be able to do the same, I read and I read and I read.

It's just after 5 pm when I finish, the closing chapter of the book ringing around in my mind. I close my eyes and take it all in, words imprinted on the back of my eyelids, that labyrinth Paige spoke of so clear to me now. Before I knew Paige I just existed, never really paying heed to anything other than the names on my list.

And I did this for centuries.

I never questioned the corner the Cosmos put me in, aimlessly drifting along, taking and taking and taking life, without ever questioning what life really meant.

I grab my phone from where I threw it on my bed earlier and ring Paige. I have to talk to her; I have to know if she figured a way out of the labyrinth. It rings and rings and she doesn't answer. I stand up and pace the length of my room, Miles' words circling around and around like a siren in my mind, aware of nothing but the downward spiral of my thoughts. Sounding irrational and unreasonable, I mentally curse Paige for not answering – how can she fill me with all these thoughts and then not be here to answer them?

Knowing I shouldn't, but being unable to stop myself anyway, I conjure thoughts of Paige and let the Cosmos whisk me away to her.

Chapter Thirty-Nine

Paige

I wake with a start, the harsh vibration of my phone pulling me out of what was a pleasant sleep. Blurry remembrances of my dream surface and a feeling of longing so potent it's almost painful. It's only once the blur of my dream fades that I realise I must have fallen asleep reading – one minute I was in the throes of Heathcliff's anguish, the next I was dreaming of dark eyes and hair, lips that taste like devastation. I grab my phone off the coffee table, noting that time has slipped away from me and it's now five o'clock. As if called forth from my dream, Lawrence's name flashes on my screen. I stare at the name, my heart racing, wondering what he could want. As I go to accept the call, it stops ringing, my hesitation at answering my own pitiful downfall. I flick to our string of messages, typing an apology for missing his call. As I type, little bubbles appear, as though Lawrence is also messaging. I wait for his message to come through.

I wait.

I wait.

Nothing.

Five minutes pass and still nothing, so I delete my half-penned reply and put my phone back on the table. I won't waste my time waiting around for anyone. Even if my heart did sink a little when he never showed up for our presentation. And sank again these past few weeks after having heard nothing from him. But I'm better than that. I'm better than a lonely girl waiting for the boy she likes to notice her. The fact that I now have a date lined up with Ari in less than two hours shows that. Not that I'm using Ari to make a point, I have nothing to prove. I guess it just feels good to know that someone is interested in me and it's nice to fill my time with things other than words between pages and fictional worlds.

Knowing that I'll need to leave about quarter to six, I have plenty of time to get ready. Having already showered, it will just be a case of throwing some clothes on and deciding what to do with my hair. It's a Saturday, which typically means afternoons spent cleaning my little two-floor apartment, a chore I've come to loathe. Even though it's small, I'm so meticulous that the task seems to take hours upon hours. But seeing as I only have about half an hour, I decide to leave it for another day. Missing one day of housework won't kill anybody, whereas the thought of doing it now might just kill my soul. Having fallen asleep mid-page, I read until the end of my chapter then head upstairs.

My hair is a mass of waves, the multi-tonal brown different shades depending on the light. With extra time to get ready than I'd normally take, I make the extra effort to straighten my hair. Because my natural hair curls in subtle waves, my hair looks that much longer straight. Looking in the mirror I almost don't look like myself, my hair a straight blanket covering my shoulders. I pull on some high-waisted flared jeans, a black lace corset and my leather jacket. With Ari being of an average height, I opt for flat, black trainers, to avoid towering over him. Another thing I can't help but dislike. The person I date is meant to make me feel delicate and dainty, but Ari's short height could quite easily make me feel like a giant, a veritable monstrosity of a girl with my above-average height! At least the bulk of his muscles makes up for what he lacks vertically, if you're into that kind of thing at least. I chide myself for being so picky and make my way downstairs, telling myself that I will have a good time tonight as though it's my own personal mantra.

Keys and phone in hand, and all electrical appliances turned off, I head out the door, only to walk into a wall. I look up in confusion and find a wall of black. The further my eyes travel, I realise that the black wall is actually a casual black t-shirt, and attached to said t-shirt, is a face I've dreamed of: Lawrence.

"Paige", he says. And that one word conjures up interminable images of his lips on mine and his hands tangled in my hair. "There's no escaping the labyrinth".

Chapter Forty

Lawrence

"There's no escaping the labyrinth", I say again, "because the labyrinth is life, and the only way out of it is death". She stares at me like I've lost my mind and I'm not entirely sure that she's wrong.

"Lawrence", she says, my name like it's both her favourite word and her worst nightmare. Only then do I take in her appearance. Her hair looks different and she's dressed up as though she's about to go out. I didn't knock, she was already on her way out when I appeared outside her door. She's busy. Heart dropping in my chest like a stone, I take a step back, allowing her to shut her front door and lock it behind her. "I'm just on my way out," she finally speaks, voicing what is now so painfully obvious to me.

"Sorry", I mumble, but I'm not sorry at all. "The labyrinth Paige, I need to know if you found another way out of it?", I ask, desperation lacing my tone.

"Like you said, there's no way out of it", and she looks sad as she says it, achingly so. "Did you really come here just to ask me that?", and I catch an undercurrent of hope in her voice.

"And to return your book", I look down at my empty hands. "But it appears as though I've forgotten it".

"You can return it another time", she smiles, trying to edge her way around me, "I'm just on my way out", she repeats.

"Yeah sure", I nod. We walk down the path from her apartment in silence, her body angled away from me. Even though we've walked in silence before, it's never been uncomfortable. Where once it was peaceful, now it's filled with all the words I find myself unable to say.

"Can we talk?", I start to say as she speaks over me.

"You didn't show up". She stops walking and turns towards me. "You didn't come to the presentation. I had to do it alone. Without you". Reprimand and disappointment rise to the surface, a newfound confidence steels her backbone as she looks me in the eye. "I thought we had the start of something good".

"We did, our project was good", I flounder, my heart racing at the accusation in her tone.

"I'm not talking about the project Lawrence". Every time I hear my name on her lips, my stomach drops just that bit more. "I'm talking about us. Me and you".

"Us?", I question.

"Yeah", she grounds out, waiting for me to speak. And I feel sick to my stomach because I thought we could have been something good too. That's exactly why I didn't show. But I can't tell her that, I can't tell her anything. She stares at me, the silence thick with hope and disappointment.

"Right", she says, "I have to go, I'm meeting someone soon", and the vague way she says that calls forth images of the blond, muscle machine she's been spending time with.

"A date?", I blurt out, even though I have no right to ask. My stomach sinks further, if such a thing is even possible, and I know that if I had been human, and better equipped with emotions, I would be happy for her. But I'm not. I'm just that selfish. It takes longer to be a good person than simply waking up one day, drowning in humanity.

"Yes Lawrence, a date", she sighs. "Don't worry about giving me the book back", she smiles sadly. I start to speak but she speaks over me. "It's yours", and with that, she unlocks her car, not looking at me once. I'm still standing on the street outside her home, her car getting smaller the further she drives. Hoping and hoping she might wave in her rear-view mirror, or better yet, turn the car around and come back to me.

But she doesn't.

The sky turns a dusky shade of black before I convince myself to move. Before, I would have faded away and got on with the task of reaping all my other souls. But now? I let my feet carry me away from her drive, walking everywhere and nowhere at once. Walking, for the first time in my existence, without aim, without purpose.

Chapter Forty-One

Lawrence

Hours later and my feet hurt from wandering aimlessly. My stomach feels hollow with thoughts of Paige on her date, thoughts whirring around and around, imagining what she could be doing with someone else. Without me. I know I have no right, but I feel sick thinking about her kissing him, him making her laugh. It's my own fault, fuck if I don't know that, but it doesn't change how I feel.

A tingling sensation creeps up my neck that I can't ignore; the next soul on my list beckoning me to do my duties no matter my futile attempts at ignoring them. I close my eyes and follow that sensation, the grey streets around me giving way to cobblestone and lilting violins. Opening my eyes, I see a sea of round, metal tables and candlelight, couples holding hands and drinking wine as if they have all the time in the world. Across the road from outside the restaurant is a stretch of green grass, lit by soft streetlamps. And that is where my next victim is. I make my way over to the grass and take in the words of those around me. Reapers are expected to know every language that exists, so it doesn't take me long to parse out the French and understand what they're saying. On a picnic blanket on the grass, a tall, blond male sits hunched over the prone form of a petite female. As I get closer, I can see the small features of the woman's face: a round shape with a slightly pointed chin, a straight nose that turns up at the end, small lips that could have once been red but are now tinged blue as the life seeps out of her. I stand behind the blond male who mourns the loss of his sweetheart. His head slowly turns to look over his shoulder, as if he can sense my unearthly presence behind him.

"Tu me manques, Celie", he whispers, pressing his lips to her forehead, "tu va me manquer ma copine". I startle back at his words, the meaning behind them hitting me right in the centre of my chest. *I miss you, Celie. I will miss you baby.* That is the literal translation, but it means so much more than that in its original language. It means you are lacking from me. And as I stand watching the poor man stroke his fingers along the cheek of my victim, the time away from Paige comes back to me in a rush. I have felt an ache without her, some indescribable hollowness that this grieving man has put into words for me: *you are lacking from me. Paige is lacking from me.*

"Is it time?", a quiet, wary voice pulls me from my morose realisation. Startled, I look up and see the shimmery soul of the dead girl standing to my right.

"It is", I nod, reaching my hand towards her. Shadows under her eyes and sickly pallor to her skin suggest that she hasn't been well for a while. That her death was something she was expecting.

"Mikel, he'll be okay, won't he?", she cries silently, her hand resting on his shoulder as if in farewell. Not having it in me to lie, I stay silent. She kisses his cheek and then takes my offered hand, letting me whisk her away to The Beyond.

As I watch the light that is her soul float away into its afterlife, Mikel's words repeat on a loop inside my head.

You are lacking from me.

Chapter Forty-Two

Paige

I don't know what came over me to voice what I had to Lawrence, but it was true, it did seem like we could have had something good. At least it did to me. I'm tired of shying away from my feelings to make other people more comfortable. Life is too short and I am better than that. I thought if I wasn't going to see him again, then at least I could be honest. But it isn't what I said that keeps replaying in my head as I drive to meet Ari, it's the desperation in his voice, the way his body seemed to shake with it when he asked me about the labyrinth. *The labyrinth Paige, I need to know if you found another way out of it?* That question has plagued me since I first read the book. Death being the way out of this labyrinth we call life has always given me comfort. But hearing the distress in Lawrence's voice, I wonder if I've been wrong. Why should we have to die to ease our suffering, to escape the chaos of life?

I let my thoughts turn and turn, the miles of road between my home and the bar dissolving away between my churning thoughts. My conversation with Lawrence has put me about five minutes behind time. My phone, which sits on a magnet on my dashboard, lights up with Ari messaging to say he's arrived. Not one to text and drive, I leave it unanswered, knowing I'll be there in about ten minutes anyway. As I pull up in the car park, I see Ari standing outside, wearing a tight white shirt and skinny jeans. Since it's just after six, parking is free, so I lock my car up and make my way over the short distance towards Ari.

Even though Ari has never really taken me as the hugging type, he leans in for a quick hug, his arm lingering on my back for longer than I'm comfortable with.

"Hey'" he says, as he opens the door for me. Ever the gentleman.

"Hey", I nod back, shucking my jacket off as the heat from the bar envelops me in a comfortable haze.

"Don't tell me what you want, I'll surprise you", Ari winks, a sudden bravado taking over. He walks over to the bar whilst I take a seat at a table in the corner, secluded away from the consumption of public eyes. I let my eyes roam as I wait for Ari to return, tuning in on the finer details of the place. The overall vibe here is relatively modern but hidden beneath that urban façade are small rustic nuances of comfort. Underneath every table is a woven rug, dyed a myriad of colours, making the steel-backed chairs that accompany the tables somewhat sterile and unforgiving. Surrounding each window are strung fairy lights, twinkling in the breeze from the open door. I've always preferred vintage to modern, but as modern designs go, I don't completely hate the style here.

Ari returns with two small whiskey glasses filled with brown liquid upon heaps and heaps of ice.

"Whiskey on the rocks for you'" Ari announces with a wink, placing the drink in front of me. Didn't he realise I was driving? There's no way I can drink all this.

"Ahh, thanks", I smile, taking a sip, trying to hide my cringe as the strong liquid practically burns my entire oesophagus. Ari too takes a sip from his drink, giving me time to study him, really study him, in a way separate from that of a platonic work friendship. As he sets his glass back on the table, he licks his lips with his tongue, eyeing me with sedate green eyes. He clenches his jaw, his face turning slightly red, as though trying to suppress a cough. His reaction being something similar to mine after just one sip of the whiskey makes me think he picked the drink thinking it would impress me, rather than being something he actually wanted. Needless to say, I am not impressed.

"Thanks for joining me tonight. I've wanted to ask you out for a while, but I wasn't sure if you'd be interested", Ari smiles at me and the sincerity in his smile washes away the slight distaste from moments ago.

"Thanks for asking me", I reply. We talk for a while and Ari tells me more about himself, telling me things I already knew from working with him. Like how he has three sisters and two cats. And things I didn't, like his crazy fascination with sharks and his desire to one day swim with them. I couldn't help but be endeared by that, that wild edge so at odds with his rather bland personality. He asks me to tell him more about myself and I don't know where to begin. What parts of myself do I want to share with him? What parts does he deserve to know? I tell him about the books I've been reading and he nods along in interest. But I can see the slight glaze that comes across his eyes, my passion for reading lost on him. And I know I shouldn't compare, but the desperation *Looking for Alaska* brought forth in Lawrence is so startlingly in comparison to the ennui Ari feels sitting opposite me. I stop talking, taking tiny sips of my drink, craving water to wash the acrid taste away. I excuse myself to the bar to grab some water and Ari nips to the toilet. Back in less than five minutes, Ari continues to talk about himself but the words don't register. My mind has now moved out of the bar and is lingering back on my driveway with Lawrence, lingering on the words I hoped he would say, but didn't.

"Shall we get another?", Ari asks, his question pulling me out of my thoughts.

"I probably shouldn't as I'm driving and I have work tomorrow". I feel guilty at the disappointment that crosses Ari's face but he nods all the same.

"Sure, no problem. I get that". I stand and he follows my lead, racing ahead to open the door for me on our way out.

"I had a really nice time", he says and I'm suddenly thrown into a panic as he steps closer to me, the unwanted reality of what's about to happen dawning on me before I get a chance to react. He leans in and kisses me, placing his hand on my cheek clumsily. My body responds whilst my mind is in stasis, moving my lips in time with his, the soft press of them against my own not entirely unpleasant, but lacking the warmth and headiness of romance. Ari steps away and my entire body sighs with relief, glad that the kiss is over. If only so I can get back in my car and analyse the entire thing, from start to finish; from what I felt to what those feelings mean.

"Text me when you get home", Ari smiles, touching my arm with his hand. He walks me to my car. I can see he wants to kiss me again, so I jump in quickly, avoiding any other advances. I watch as he walks out of the car park, just sitting in the silence of my car before turning the engine on. I sit for five minutes and then ten, trying to gather the energy to put my belt on and drive.

As I pull out of the car park, the dark night sky surrounding me, the solitude of the night washes over me. I leave the music off and just drive. There's something about driving at night, the night sky flying past my windows, interrupted only by streetlamps and building lights, the solid concrete of the road rushing underneath my tires.

I drive and drive and soon find myself home, walking through my apartment door, getting undressed and ready for bed. All of this is done automatically, as though on autopilot. Even though I know as I fall asleep, the last thoughts on my mind should be of Ari, how sweet he was by running ahead to open the door for me, the soft touch of his lips on mine, Ari is not who I think of. Instead, like a loop around my mind, Lawrence's words echo through me, chasing me into my dreams long after I've fallen asleep.

There's no escaping the labyrinth ... The labyrinth Paige, I need to know if you found another way out of it?

Chapter Forty-Three

Paige

I wake up before seven to get ready for work. The weather seems a lot cooler today than yesterday, so I throw on some black joggers instead of shorts, the bright yellow t-shirt all lifeguards are tormented to wear, and a red sweatshirt. Once I've brushed my teeth, I head downstairs and grab a pot noodle for lunch and throw it in my bag. I fill up my water bottle and make a coffee in my flask for the short drive to the leisure centre. I turn all the lights off, lock up after myself and head to my car.

I arrive at work in under ten minutes, one of the perks of living near the leisure centre. Another perk is that it also pays quite well; even though I've got a long shift today, I'll have been paid a decent amount by the end to make it worth it. As I walk into the building, I try to muster the energy required for the day. I sign in and look at the sign-in sheet to see who else is in for the day. The only other person that I generally speak to at work apart from Ari, Lillith, and Brando, is Willis, who is also on shift today. Saying hello to the people behind reception, I go to the staff room to put my things into my locker and head onto pool.

The day passes with relative ease, hours spent on pool watching people swim broken up by cleaning and reading on my breaks. There's only an hour and a half left of my shift before I know it; the last hour of the shift is spent deep cleaning. It's therapeutic in a way, the loud whirring of the power washer and cool splash of water on my ankles, a peaceful melody. I move the machine down the floor of the changing rooms, the left-to-right motion of the machine hypnotic in its regularity. Once the floor is cleaned, I do a final spot check and wipe the day's dirt off the mirrors in the bathrooms and complete any last-minute checks that need doing. Willis comes to help me as I'm finishing up, a smirk on his face.

"So I heard you went out with Ari last night", he winks at me as though he knows something I don't.

"Yeah", I say passively, not really sure where this conversation is heading.

"Is he like your boyfriend now then?", that smirk stays on his face and all I want to do is take the cloth I'm using to wipe it off.

"No, I wouldn't so say", I nod, hoping we can now drop the conversation. Willis frowns as though something I've said doesn't make sense.

"Maybe you should make sure he knows that", the smirk now thankfully gone is replaced by his raised eyebrows. And I feel as if I'm missing something.

"What?", I question. He holds up his hands, taking a step away from me.

"Not my place man, just saying", and with that, he takes the cloth and cleaning spray from my hands and walks out of the changing rooms into reception. Shaking my head with annoyance, I wash my hands in the sink and head to the staff room to get my stuff. As I walk back out into reception, Willis and the other guys are whispering about something. And I know I'm being paranoid, but I've got it in my head that they're talking about me and Ari, especially after what Willis just said to me. This kind of schoolgirl paranoia is exactly why I've always been hesitant to go out with anyone from work in the first place. I give the guys a quick wave goodbye and then head to my car, looking forward to an evening by myself.

My phone goes off as I get in my car and I see a text from Ari asking if I'm free later. I sigh inwardly, wanting to spend the night in by myself and now also not wanting to deal with the awkward conversation that I'm sure to have in the coming days. It's not that I don't like Ari, he really is a nice person. It's just that I don't see him in a romantic way, and the kiss last night only cemented those feelings. I groan as I pull out of the car park, my belly already in knots thinking about that conversation. And it isn't a big deal, we only went out once, but I just feel bad because no one wants to be rejected. It just doesn't feel good.

Once I get home, I drop Ari a text asking him if he's free the day after tomorrow. I have book club tomorrow and don't want to feel like I have to rush that to then see Ari in the afternoon. I also kind of want to put off this conversation a little while longer, even if that does make me a bit of a coward. He texts back and suggests going for a walk. With that conversation banked for now, I head upstairs and take a shower. As the warm water washes over me, my thoughts wander to Lawrence and I find myself replaying our interaction yesterday over and over again. Stepping out of the shower and wrapping a big fluffy towel around myself, I sit on the edge of the bed and contemplate texting Lawrence. Even though I know I shouldn't give him the time of day after not showing up for our project presentation, the devil on my shoulder tells me that one text surely won't hurt. Will it?

'Did you not like the end of the book?'

I ask and lay my phone back on my bed whilst I dry off and get into my pyjamas. This week's pjs consists of a particularly oversized t-shirt with long slipper socks. Dressed and ready to settle into bed for an hour before making dinner, I light some candles and put my reading light on. I hear my phone go off just as I've climbed into bed and my heart does a weird little flip in my chest. Lawrence replies with a long message, saying how he didn't just like the book, but he *loved* it. He's then written a paragraph of questions, both about this so-called labyrinth, but also plot details he doesn't quite understand. I bite my lip - the fury I felt at him for leaving me to do our presentation alone softens from the pure excitement that shines through his message. I don't think he's faking it to impress me, I think he really did enjoy reading it. If he didn't, there's no way he'd have so many thoughts about the book. Wanting to see his excitement in person, I contemplate asking him to meet up. I type and re-type and type the message over and over, but every time I go to hit send, some gut instinct pulls my finger back at the last second. Instead, I reply with a quick 'glad you liked it' text, silence my phone and put it on the table beside my bed.

Heathcliff calls my name and the next hour rushes by with epic scenes of romance between Catherine and Heathcliff and I practically throw my book out the window, screaming at them to get their lives together and confess their love for each other already. I take a break to cook a quick cheese and mushroom omelette, then jump back into bed and spend the night cursing Cathy and Heathcliff's inability to communicate and consequently mourn the great love they never had a chance to share.

As I'm brushing my teeth, getting ready to go to sleep, I see the silent flash of Lawrence's name appear on my phone. Not thinking twice about it, I accept the call, wanting to know what reason he could have to call me now.

"Hey", I pick up on the second ring.

"Hey", Lawrence whispers back and even though it's only one word, it's the best one I've heard all day.

Chapter Forty-Four

Lawrence

I walked for hours after leaving reaping Celie's soul, the cry of other wayward souls awaiting my presence now secondary to the urgency to make things right with Paige. I walked until the dark sky became smudged with yellow, the sun slowly making its appearance in the sky. Only when I felt as though my feet couldn't walk anymore did I head back to HQ, planning on a shower, and then I didn't know what. Just as I reached the front doors of HQ, a soft tingle starting behind my eyes and travelling all the way to the bottom of my feet, pulled me up short. Quickly pulling my list of souls from my pocket, I saw the bold name flash at the top, highlighting another soul ready to be reaped. I let the Universe guide me and went on my way to see my next soul.

That is where I've spent the rest of this day, sitting in the corner of the white-walled hospital room, watching the family of the deceased stare blankly at the now-empty bed. When I came for Maggie's soul, an old woman in her ninth decade of life, she grabbed my hand eagerly, thoughts of The Beyond filling her mind with peace and rest. As I guided her spirit to The Beyond, I heard her whisper the same name over and over: Derek, Derek, Derek. A part of me feels relief at knowing she'll be reunited with whoever this Derek is to her. The other part of me has sat here for hours, tormenting myself with the tear-stained faces of the family she has left behind. Nurses frequently come in and out of the room, clearing it of all the unnecessary items, dead flowers, paper cards and dirty bed sheets.

I don't know what the time is, or for how long I've sat here for when I notice that the bereaved family is no longer in the room. Five hours? Six? Longer? The way the time has flown by without much recollection of what's occurred troubles me. Losing hours at a time, wasted sitting in my own thoughts, is unbecoming of a Reaper. Where usually I am fastidious in how I proceed throughout the day, I have become remiss in my duties, more concerned with what my reaping does to the humans left behind, than the souls I actually ferry. *What is happening to me?*

I walk out of the hospital on my two feet, scanning around at all the empty beds and grieving people. The cloud of grief is broken up by rays of sunlight as I watch smiles cross the faces of patients as they receive good news or as parents take their newborn babies home. I think most newborn babies look rather ugly; their faces all scrunched up with no real features yet to speak of. But the joy and pride radiating from new moms and dads makes the whole thing seem rather nice. Following some newly minted parents out the front doors of the hospital, I feel my phone buzz in my pocket. It's Paige. I read her message with nervous anticipation, her name alone enough to evoke a vivid hope and yearning I am now only just getting used to. She's asking about what I thought of the book, and I pen a reply immediately, needing her to answer the questions and thoughts that have since popped into my head regarding the overall plot but also small nuances throughout.

I make my way back to HQ for the second time today whilst awaiting her reply. My phone buzzes as I'm walking up the steps and into the foyer. Paige's simple, one sentence makes my stomach drop. It's barely a reply. Trying to mask my disappointment, I slide my phone back into my pocket and head to Anchor's office to make a report. I get there and his door is closed, so I wait outside like the good little penitent I'm no longer sure I am.

"Thank you Mattias", Anchor nods as he ushers out one of the lower-level Reapers. From filing away death reports to making sure the training room is stocked with supplies, Mattias, along with others, is normally responsible for overseeing that the administration duties of HQ are all taken care of. He must have just finished an inventory meeting or such with Anchor. Nodding his greeting, Mattias heads left out of Anchor's office, making his way to the administrative offices on the second floor.

"Ah, Law, so good to see you", and now it is I being ushered into Anchor's office. "All good things to report, I hope". For one normally prone to fits of anger and a general stern disposition, Anchor seems all too friendly for my liking. Unease uncoils like a deadly snake in my belly.

"Yes and no sir'" I reply, standing with my arms clasped behind my back as Anchor takes a seat behind his desk.

"Speak", he commands, a frown furrowing the small space between his eyebrows.

"Maggie Whilts passed on this morning and the reaping was a success. Celie Lantyrn and Malcom Strong were also collected successfully". I sense that mentioning the confusion with Paige's name getting further down my list won't end well for me, so decide to keep that fact to myself.

"Anything else?", Anchors asks, almost as if he can sense that I'm hiding something.

"No. Nothing at all". What is it humans say? Plausible deniability?

"Well", Anchor pauses, clearing his throat. "If that is all, Law, you are dismissed". He doesn't offer me the same courtesy he showed Mattias, leaving me to walk out of his office by myself. I guess I should start investigating this whole Paige situation before it gets even worse, where I'll no doubt be forced to confide the mess to Anchor.

I walk to my room on the fourth floor, closing the door behind me. Only when I'm alone do I take my phone out of my pocket and hit call, welcoming the sound of Paige's voice.

"Hey", she answers on the second ring. Surely the best way to investigate this whole situation is by spending time with her again?

"Hey", I grin, knowing I'm treading down the road to my own demise. And not one part of me is remotely bothered by that thought at all.

Chapter Forty-Five

Lawrence

I stayed up talking to Paige for hours. The sky turned dark and the moon shone, then the sky turned from dusky grey to a delicate pink as the sun came out behind the clouds. We spoke about books; not just Looking for Alaska, but other books that Paige has read or is reading. She told me about her newfound passion for rock climbing and how she woke up sad the morning before last with no reason, this unexplainable heaviness clouding her thoughts. That's why she wanted to go out with her friends from work, as a distraction. And I felt honoured that she'd confided something so intimate and raw with me. Honoured.

A loud knock on my door startles me; I must have dropped off without even realising it. I grab my phone to see if I'm still on the line to Paige, but it just shows a good morning text from her instead. My heart does a little somersault seeing her name flash on my screen.

"Law, are you in there?", Elodie knocks again and my stomach sinks. I quickly make the bed and try and make myself presentable. Reapers don't sleep; if Elodie caught my drifting off, I don't even know how she'd react, but it wouldn't be good.

"Yeah", I open the door, trying not to look suspicious.

"Have you been sleeping?", she frowns, that worry I saw in her face the other day in the training room making an appearance. "Your clothes are all rumpled and your hair is a mess". She tries to pull out the crinkles in my t-shirt but to no avail.

"Let me just change my top". I hurry to my wardrobe and pull out another black t-shirt. Not caring that the door is still open and Elodie has a view of my bare chest and back. I pull my crinkled shirt over my head.

"Law, what is that?", Elodie frantically crosses the space between us, just as I'm pulling my clean top over my head. With my eyes covered by the material of my shirt, I don't know what she's talking about.

"Here", her cold hand touches the middle of my chest, where a heart would be if I were human. I flinch. The sensation of her cold hand on my chest is startling. Where normally the iciness of her touch wouldn't affect me, because I too have ice-cold skin, today it almost takes my breath away. Not lingering on what that could mean, I quickly untuck my head from the opening in the shirt and look down at Elodie's hand.

"What is it? I can't see El, your hand is in the way". Elodie removes her hand and I feel a cold dread seep through my veins. Where her hand was, I now see a reddish-purple bruise, starting from the top of my left ribcage and ending just above where my belly button would be.

"It must have happened whilst I was reaping", I explain away, even though I have no recollection of how that came to be. The look on Elodie's face screams that she doesn't believe me, but I don't know what else to tell her. If I'm honest, the sight of that bruise on my skin is more than a little worrying. She steps away from me, something like admonishment on her face as she opens her mouth to speak.

"What did you come here for", I interrupt, not wanting her to make me feel worse about the bruise, and the fact that I'd fallen asleep, which I've done more than once in the last few weeks. That in itself is enough to cause a spiral of anxiety. My breathing rate picks up but I try to calm it. If Elodie weren't here, distracting me, I imagine the anxiety flooding my system, my thoughts spiralling, my breathing erratic, would be what humans describe as a panic attack. Instead, her voice pulls me out of that spiral, my breathing slows and I pull myself together.

"Anchor's called an emergency meeting in the training room. Everyone is to report there in ten minutes. Didn't you hear the announcement go off?", she questions me. And damn if I didn't. I was too busy losing myself in the blissful unconsciousness of sleep.

"I've only just got back from finishing an assignment", I say, the lie rolling off my tongue with little effort. "It wasn't an easy job, hence the ruffled appearance". Perhaps saying the latter seems a little too suspicious but I walk out of my bedroom before Elodie can argue.

We make our way in silence to the training room levels below. What was once a rather companionable silence is now filled with an uneasy tension. I step into the elevator that will take us straight into the training room, the silver doors so shiny they show our reflections. The lift starts to descend, a light ping echoing in the metal chamber as we pass by the different levels. Out of nowhere, Elodie slams her hand on the stop button, pulling the lift to a harsh stop. If it weren't for our Reaper senses, the two of us would have ended up flat on the floor as the lift comes to an abrupt halt.

"Elodie, what are you doing?", I question, confused and now somewhat anxious. "We're going to be late".

"We need to talk Law. We can't put this off any longer". She looks at me and waits, as if I'm supposed to know what exactly it is we need to *talk* about. I stare back at her, unflinching in my mission not to break the silence first. Elodie sighs and I know I've won.

"We need to talk about you... what's happening to you".

"Nothing's happening to me", I deny because even if something was, I have no clue what it could even be.

"I know we're friends Law, but I still have a duty outside of that.

I've been around a bit longer than you, I know the signs. I've seen it before".

"Signs of what?", I frown, not sure what she's getting at.

"Of humanity".

"That's not -"

"It is Law", she interrupts, placing her hand on my shoulder delicately. "I don't know if it's being with your charge Paige, or something else, but you're changing. I can see it in the tired lines on your face and your hesitancy to even be here". I shake my head, starting to deny it, but realise that I can't.

"Elodie", I begin.

"No, Lawrence, there's nothing you can say. That mark on your chest, you know what it means, even if you pretend you don't". *But do I know? It's just a bruise, I tell myself.* Subconsciously, my hand drifts to my chest, hovering over where that bruise is beneath my shirt. My stomach lurches, a faint pulse trickling through my fingers. *Da-dum, da-dum.*

It can't be.

Putting that beat beneath my fingers down to adrenaline, I dismiss what I feel and what Elodie is trying to say. I step around her, pressing the button to start the elevator again.

"You're wrong El", I turn to her as I stand back by her side. "Wrong", I reaffirm.

"I wish I was", Elodie sighs, and I catch her watching me even once I've turned away from her. She watches me from the corner of her eye as we dutifully enter the training hall and stand in line, awaiting Anchor's brief. Watching me as though my time as Reaper is slowly coming to an end.

Chapter Forty-Six

Lawrence

"Something is happening throughout the cosmos", Anchor begins once all Reapers are lined up, a sea of blank faces waiting to hear his decree. "Something that has not been seen in thousands of years", he pauses, letting his words sink in, each word a drop of rain falling onto our heads, seeping into our systems and causing mild panic. "I am not at liberty to discuss the specifics, but this thing will be the explanation as to why some of your lists might be shifting around". A murmur passes through the hall like a wave as we turn to our peers in confusion. "As long as you carry on reaping the souls in the exact order they appear on your list, as and when you consult it, then all will be fine".

Without giving much more information, Anchor dutifully bows and makes his way out of the training hall and back to the recesses of his office. As he reaches the door, he scans the crowd and I get the distinct impression that he is looking at me; his eyes dark holes boring into me with untamed anger. "Elodie", he shouts to the crowd and I watch Elodie turn her head in his direction, "a word please". Not waiting for her to reach him, he leaves the room and the hall erupts in conversation. I make towards the exit, planning on following Elodie but she gives me a quick shake of her head over her shoulder and I feel myself pause.

She doesn't want me with her.

Letting Elodie walk away, I consult my list of souls and see that Paige's name is now right at the bottom of my list. The writing shimmers as the names start to shuffle around, Paige's name now moving up a place. I exhale in relief, knowing that I still have more time before I must do what I cannot fathom: take her soul. Margot Zimmerman is the name at the top of my list, her name flashing red, signalling that her time is almost here. I let instinct guide me towards her, walking out of HQ and out into the dreary day, rain soaking the pavement and now my clothes before I've even made it ten steps. Like when Elodie touched my chest, the cold feel of the water on my skin is startling; the delicate patter of ice against my face, tantalising; my skin coming alive under the feel of the heavens raining down around me. I focus on that pull in my chest, the bond that all Reapers' share with their charges, and make my way past the school building down the road from HQ. I walk past the coffee shop I first took Paige to. I walk and I walk and I walk. Listening to the hum in my chest, I walk aimlessly. I can tell Margot isn't ready yet, so I walk without direction until such time that she is.

The salty smell of food nearby pulls me out of my directionless walk, and my feet carry me closer to the source of it, without my mind even realising it. As I round the corner, a little restaurant sits on the corner, customers sitting outside, despite the rain, under striped canopies surrounded by large, leafy plants and colourful flowers. Not needing to eat for sustenance but intrigued by the smell and the way my stomach seems to growl in response to it, I make my way over.

"Table for one", a young girl with brown skin and jet-black hair asks me. White shirt and black trousers are mostly covered by a striped apron that matches the canopies outside.

"Yes please", I nod. A buzz of, dare I say it, excitement runs through me as I'm escorted to a table near the window, greeted by a view of the flowers and street outside.

"Can I get you anything to drink?", she smiles at me, the slight twang of an accent becoming more pronounced the longer I hear her speak.

"Just water, please", I say.

"No problem. Here's the menu for you and I'll go fetch your water". I take the menu off her, her warm hand a pleasant sensation against my damp skin. The menu is extensive, crammed full of food I've never even heard before. And it hits me then, that I shouldn't even be here. I didn't need food; frankly human food has always had an almost cardboard, bland taste to me because Reapers lack the tastebuds humans have which makes the experience of food that much more enjoyable.

And yet, as I sit here, my eyes roaming over the different options on offer, the smell of food wafting in from the kitchen, a delicious invitation, I find that it goes beyond just wanting to see what the food tastes like. *I need to.* Much in the same way I had to know what it felt like to taste Paige on my lips, this hunger for food surpasses simply satiating a visceral hunger; it's a hunger of my very being, at needing to have yet another human experience of eating food so good it nourishes one's soul. Elodie's face appears in my mind, her words echoing in my mind; her worry no longer seeming so unreasonable. Reapers don't need, we don't hunger. It isn't in our mandate to function in any capacity except to reap souls.

But here I am. The smell of good food around me, feeling a nervous excitement and contentedness just being in the here and now. And this peace is almost too good to let her worries bother me. It's exquisite.

"And what can I get for you", the waitress grins down at me, her cheeriness so contagious I feel a smile tugging at the corners of my own mouth.

"I'd like to try the spaghetti carbonara please", I say, "as well as the garlic bread, breaded chicken and cheese sticks". It feels like I've ordered the entire menu, but my mouth took over my brain, listing off each item my eyes came across, the thrill of just sitting here taking over.

"Hungry, huh?", she laughs.

"You wouldn't believe it", I grin back.

"I'll go pop your order into the kitchen and it will be done soon. Anything else you need for now?"

"Nothing at all". She walks away and I spend the next twenty minutes people watching. I take a sip of water, the ice cubes causing condensation to drip down the glass. People mill past the restaurant, zooming by on their way to work or to meet friends. And for once, it's nice to be separate from that chaos, just sitting here and drinking in the busy outside world. I feel settled in a way I can't say I ever have before. My job now causes me distress; taking souls but never giving back all these centuries, is finally taking its toll on me. And being with Paige makes my body hum in a way I cannot settle - her presence brings me to life in a way that sets my skin on fire. It's hard to feel settled when you feel as though you're burning apart from the inside out. So, this time here, to myself? Fuck, I don't want it to end.

"Here's your food", the waitress places multiple plates down in front of me, and my mouth waters as the rich smell of the food makes its way to my nose.

"Thank you", I say, really meaning it. Her serving me food has more meaning than she could ever know.

"Let me know if you need anything else". I don't waste a second once she's walked away, spinning whirls of spaghetti around my fork like a carbohydrate tornado. The first taste of the spaghetti has me delving for more. I devour what's in front of me with no hesitation. And I can't decide what I enjoy more, the greasy Chinese food I had with Paige, or the hearty, comforting taste of pasta. Placing my fork down, I pull apart of piece of garlic bread, the taste so decadent I take a swig of water before continuing.

And just like that, I lose myself in the flavours in front of me, the crispy breaded chicken adding texture to the softness of the pasta. I'm full before I know it. I look at the relatively empty dishes in front of me and find myself impressed by how much food I actually managed to put away. It really was too good to not eat as much as I could. What's nicer than the food is the mindlessness I've felt; getting lost in new tastes has distracted me from the anxiety caused by the changes I've noticed within myself, the pain I feel at losing Paige, and the rebellion I feel towards my duty as a Reaper.

For this hour alone, I have been able to exist just as Lawrence. Nothing more, nothing less. Just me. And that feeling, perhaps more than anything, is something I think I'll always crave now.

Reality beckons me in no time at all as if the thoughts of gratitude were a herald to bring me crashing back down to earth. The soft intuition known to all Reapers when one of their charges dies goes off in my head. Margot Zimmerman is finally ready to enter The Beyond. Conjuring up money from thin air, I leave what I owe on the table and walk out the door. As my feet hit the concrete, a warm beam of sunlight falls on me, a soft kiss of comfort on my shoulder. As I spirit away to Margot, I can't help feeling as though that touch of sunlight on my skin was some sort of sign. But what sign, I don't know.

Chapter Forty-Seven

Lawrence

There's chaos when I get here, people milling about in a panicked frenzy. I'm guided by that inner voice towards my next charge. Margot is a woman, perhaps in the middle of life, her blonde hair greying slightly at the roots, faint crows-feet around her eyes, even in the slumber of death. This death, like some, isn't an easy one; it wasn't expected. She's dressed for hiking, lying lifelessly on the grassy plain at the bottom of a steep hike. Her friends mill around her, shouting her name. But to no avail. I kneel down next to her, her soul resting quietly on her knees next to her prone body. She looks around in confusion, not quite seeing me yet. But she will. They always do. I don't know what drives me, but I place my hand on her shoulder in comfort, and she finally looks my way. She takes a deep breath and I know she's realised who I am, what I represent. She shakes her head vehemently, denial drenching her spirit until it's all I can taste.

"I'm sorry", I say but I can tell she's still resistant, not wanting to accept me. Because accepting me, who I represent, means letting go of all that ties her here.

"But how, I was fine, I was just walking and then suddenly I felt this sharp pain in my head. It was so painful. And then I was here, kneeling over my body". She keeps shaking her head as she's talking, as if trying to will herself back into existence.

"I'm sorry", I repeat, not here to offer her an explanation; only here to take her soul to where it needs to go. "Come", I say. I let my hand fall from her shoulder and stand, my hand now held out towards her, beckoning her to my side.

"No, I won't go. You can't make me". Margot turns around quickly, making to run away from me. But I've trained for this and I'm quicker than her. You can't outrace Death. Before she's even managed to do a 180, my hand is on her upper arm and I start to transition, the edges of earth blurring away in favour of the grey vagueness of The Beyond.

The darkness of the Universe crowds around us, and in the distance, I can see a flurry of souls dancing towards The Beyond, the peace they will feel falls like a lull over me. But the pull I feel for Margot's soul isn't towards The Beyond, but rather The Abyss. My head whips around and I stare at Margot in disbelief. To look upon her is to see a rather unassuming individual, no defining characteristics either good or bad, no malicious undertone to her mien. Now that I'm focusing on her more intently, I can hear the soft mutter of words she repeats to herself again and again and again. Like those words will be enough to save her soul.

"It wasn't my fault, it wasn't my fault, it wasn't my fault". Even though the final judgement is above a Reaper's jurisdiction, if we look hard enough, we can see into the living transgressions of a soul. I rarely do it because the life of a soul has always seemed irrelevant to me, but now I can't help being intrigued. What did this woman do that was so terrible that she's been condemned to an afterlife with no peace? For to be sentenced to The Abyss is to know no peace, to be forever tormented by the sins you committed in life. I turn fully to her, my body squared off with hers. Locking my eyes with the sea glass ones across from me, I tune out the darkness around me and focus on her. I breathe her soul into me, for the briefest of moments, and become her.

It's nighttime and I'm in a car. It's raining so hard I struggle to see the road in front of me. Struggle to see the pavement that lines the street. Struggle to see the red stop sign. It happens so quickly. The child runs out in front of my car and I barely even press the brakes before a loud thud shudders through the vehicle. I come to a complete stop and then reverse. The broken body of a child lies in the street before me. With that broken image in mind, all I can think of are the three double vodkas I had before getting in my car tonight. All I can think about is the police breath-testing me. I reverse and then accelerate, driving around the crumpled body of the poor little boy, his small frame a retreating figure in my rearview mirror.

I gasp, stepping away from Margot, unknown hatred and anger erupting like wildfire in my veins. Silent tears run down Margot's face, as if my living the memory caused her to re-live it herself. She's shaking her head again as if she can turn back time, as if she can change the past.

She can't.

All compassion has left me in an icy wave, her early death no longer seeming unjust to me. I take a deep breath in, this time inhaling her spirit for one final time. On a long exhale, I breathe her soul into the fiery realms of The Abyss, hoping that her guilt and shame haunt her for the rest of her existence.

Never knowing such before, I let it consume me as I disappear back to earth. Away from here and the ugliness of humanity I've now been awakened to.

Chapter Forty-Eight

Paige

Staying up late talking to Lawrence felt like something my fifteen-year-old self would've done. It was like being a teenager again, feeling so tired, my eyelids could barely stay open, but also a little dizzy with the adrenaline of texting the person you fancy. I wouldn't say that I fancy Lawrence, because I'm not in school anymore, this isn't a childhood crush. But there is something about him; some instinctual part of myself is drawn to him in a way that makes my heart stutter a little in my chest and I become flustered. So maybe it's a mature version of fancying someone. All I know is that I could see something with him, something I don't think I've ever felt for anyone before. The attraction I feel for him is electric compared to the sickly watered-down flame I could barely muster when I'm with Ari.

I check my phone as I roll out of bed and see that Heidi has messaged to check that I'm still coming to book club. It's just before nine, so I have an hour to get ready and head to the coffee shop where we're meeting. I text Heidi back saying yeah and include a book meme to show how excited I am. I'm a bit nervous to be surrounded by a group of new people, but if they're as nice as Heidi is, then I'm sure I'll have a great time. I reassure myself with the fact that we'll be discussing the book so it's not like I'll have to awkwardly try and think of conversation topics and small talk. I quickly brush my teeth and pull the top half of my hair back with a scrunchy, the ends a tangled mess falling down my back. Throwing on flares and a big, cosy fleece, I put the address of the coffee shop into maps on my phone to see how long it will take to get there. It's currently saying twenty minutes so I've got plenty of time.

I head downstairs and grab *Iron Flame* off my bookshelf, running my hand over the gap where *Looking for Alaska* should be. It's become a habit of mine, but where that empty space used to fill me with painful yearning and disappointment, it now makes my stomach flip flop with excitement, thoughts of Lawrence now more hopeful than morose. Smiling to myself, I put my book in my bag and fill my water bottle up, then head out to my car. The grass on my drive crinkles underfoot, the frost coating everything in white dust, transforming the ordinary into something of awe. Cobwebs on my wing mirrors cling in dusty patterns, and the frost has made them beautiful. My car takes ten minutes to defrost so I sit inside with the heater blasting and let Heidi know I'm on my way. Windscreen just clear enough to see through, I let music wash away my growing nerves and head to book club.

***

There are six of us sitting around a large wooden table, coffees in hand and books on the table in front of us. Heidi introduced me to everyone when I walked in and Jackson, a willowy, dark-haired guy with a beanie, grabbed me a chair from another table and made room for me to sit between himself and Heidi. It was a surprise to see a mix of both males and females, since I know a lot of the craze around this book at the moment is from hysterical females, myself included. Jackson went around the table, introducing everyone and then we all ordered our coffees.

"We just need to call Lewis in and then we can start", Jackson announces and I look at Heidi quizzically.

"He's on holiday but didn't want to miss out on the discussion so we said we'd video call him in", she grins and I can't help but laugh. Talk about commitment.

"Hey everyone", Lewis shouts as Jackson stands his phone up against his now-empty mug at the end of the table. He drank his coffee like a psycho, one big gulp and it was gone. Coffee should be savoured, the experience of each sip dragged out over the space of an hour or two.

"This is Paige", Jackson points towards me and I wave awkwardly.

"Nice to meet you", I say amid a slew of hellos from everyone else.

"Shall we let Paige do the honours and begin the discussion", Jackson declares, the self-proclaimed spokesperson of the group.

"Are you sure? Doesn't someone else want to start?", I look around the group, feeling my cheeks go red from the attention of all eyes on me.

"Go for it Paige", Heidi beams. So I do. I launch into my detailed analysis of the plot and writing style, hearing grunts of disagreement and howls of approval as I gush over the male love interest and moan over boring storylines and dragged-out chapters. Everyone seems to dance around discussing the end of the book, as though it's some taboo that we dare not talk about, lest we ruin it for anyone close by who happens to be listening in.

"Are we going to talk about the end, when Xaden…",I begin, deciding that I can't bite my tongue any longer.

"Finally", Lewis shouts, "I was wondering when someone would finally bring that up. I died when I got to the last page!", he screams, and we get dirty looks off an old couple sitting across the room for Lewis' rowdy outburst. We all laugh at the same time, Lewis' outburst seeming to speak for how most of us feel about the ending.

"I thought it was obvious", Maya, a tall girl with square glasses and a short, black bob says from her chair on the other side of Heidi.

"You always say that about everything", Jackson rolls his eyes.

"I do not", Maya crosses her arms over her chest stubbornly.

"You kind of do", Heidi cajoles. "You'll notice this soon enough Paige", she says, winking at me, and I'm filled with gratitude for the ease in which they've let me into their circle and excitement at getting to do this again.

"What's the next book on the list then?", I ask as we all start to gather our things together.

"We thought we'd pick something festive, so we went for *Let it Snow*. John Green co-wrote with a few other authors", Maya says.

"I haven't heard of that one. I do like John Green though so I'm looking forward to it". I make a mental note of the book so I can order it online later.

"I think so. We normally meet every three weeks so you should have enough time to get it read", Maya smiles at me and I nod.

"Well, it was nice meeting you all and thanks again for letting me join", the last part I say to Heidi.

"Of course", Heidi exclaims, "you're part of the club now!".

We all head out of the coffee shop together and then go our separate ways. Having parked a little walk away because I wasn't sure if there was parking next to the coffee shop, I enjoy the cool fresh air against my cheeks, a stark contrast to the stuffy heat inside. I check my phone as I get to my car and am startled to see that three hours have passed so quickly. I avoided looking at my phone for the entire time I was at book club because I just wanted to enjoy and experience the present moment, rather than being on my phone, which was nice. It was refreshing. It felt like living.

***

Hours later, I am sitting in bed, the kindle version of *Let It Snow* slowly being devoured whilst I wait for the physical copy to be delivered, when my phone rings.

"Hey", I answer on the first ring, Lawrence's name on my screen doing silly things to the butterflies in my stomach.

"Paige", Lawrence drawls and I don't think I'll ever get used to the decadence of my name on his lips, "want to go for a drive?".

Chapter Forty-Nine

Lawrence

Needing to dispel the anger boiling inside me after reaping Margot's soul, I know only one way of accomplishing that: seeing Paige. But not in a maddening crowd of humans, struggling to hear her voice in the noises of those around us. Just the two of us. I honk my horn to let her know I'm outside, my anger making me obnoxious and loud. As Paige walks towards my car, I can already feel my anger slipping away, her presence a welcome balm to the cruelty of humans.

"Hey", Paige says as she slips inside, the sleeve of her sweatshirt getting caught in the door handle as she closes it behind her.

"Here, let me help", leaning across, I feel her breath on my neck as I fiddle to untangle her jumper, her body a warm presence at my side. I linger, the heat of her body a temptation to kiss her, imploring that I pull her mouth to mine as though she is my only sustenance.

"There you go", I say and place her hand on her lap, slowly returning myself to my seat. I let go of Paige's hand at the last second, pushing a wayward lock of hair behind her ear that causes a faint blush to stain the colour of her cheeks. Damn, I'm not sure I'll ever get used to the sight of that. Unable to resist, I trail my hand along her cheek, the blood rushing beneath the surface, a distant calling of what I will take away from her. Her life.

"Hey", I smile sadly, somewhat lost in thought, as I lower my hand and turn the car on.

"Are you okay?".

"Yeah, I'm fine", sighing, I relax my shoulders. I might not have been okay ten minutes ago, but now that she's here, I'm more than okay.

"So, where are we going?", she asks as I indicate and pull away from the curb, the roar of the engine almost drowning out her words.

"I don't have a destination in mind. I just kind of feel like getting lost on the road".

"It's all about the journey", she winks and I feel like I'm missing something but I smile at her anyway.

"Something like that", I shrug. We drive for minutes in silence, the woosh of the cold air against the windows the only sound.

"If you drive up towards The Hills, there's a country road to the right you can take that takes you to a little look off point", Paige tells me. "It's not far once you get on the motorway".

"So we do have a destination", I joke.

"We'll call it a check point, not the end", and fuck if I don't want this to end. I never want it to end. The road whizzes past as we fly down the motorway. With there being no other cars on the road, I pick up speed, getting that same rush from running fast during training that I do now. It's exhilarating.

"It's the next left here", Paige says and I slow the car down, the adrenaline leaving my body as the car winds down. I turn off where she indicated and we start to crawl up a gradual slope, the lights of the city twinkling below us like stars fallen from grace. The night sky in reverse sky, sprawling beneath us. If I were to open my window and reach my arm out, I feel as though I could capture the light in my palms. We creep up and up until I see a semi-circle of flattened dirt to one side, faded tire marks left behind by whoever came here last. I pull up on the dirt and park the car. I've barely turned the engine off when Paige all but jumps out of the car in eagerness.

"Come on Lawrence, come look", she beckons and I hurry after her. Like there was any chance I would never not follow her. As I move around to her side of the car, I see what all the fuss is about. From this vantage point, you can see endless trees and the lights of the city in the background. With the frost coating everything in a layer of white, it looks surreal; the distant lights glinting off the frost crystals in a way that makes the world below us seem almost hazy. Paige reaches her hand out towards the view below, her fingers skimming over the lights. From this angle, it looks as though she's captured that light in her hands, just as I thought of doing on the drive up here.

Instead of reaching out to catch the light, I catch Paige's hand instead. I turn Paige towards me and the wind whips her hair across her face, shielding it from me. I step closer and use both hands to brush her hair back over her shoulders, lowering my mouth to hers slowly, as though we have all the time in the world. It's just a touch of our lips, it's barely a kiss, but it does things to me I cannot even put into words.

"Look up Lawrence", Paige says so I do, her lips brushing my chin as she too turns her gaze to the sky.

"This high up there's less pollution so you can see the stars better", she sighs and the sight of her contentment brings a warm buzz to my body.

"It's like we're stood in the middle of the sky, surrounded by stars on all sides". Paige takes a step back from me, lifting her arms above her head and letting her head fall back even more, weightlessly. "It's like being a part of the Universe", she laughs as she spins around in a circle, getting lost in the magic of this place. And it's enchanting, watching her lose herself in feeling. She tugs on my hand and spins me around, and suddenly I'm lost too. The stars surrounding me, I tilt my head back and a laugh escapes my throat, so pure and untamed that I find my voice hoarse afterwards.

"It's like being lost in the vastness", I whisper to Paige as we come to a standstill, both looking back out over the view below, "like falling into oblivion and never coming back". Paige smiles at me and fuck if I don't feel like the ground is moving under my feet and I fall into that oblivion I just spoke of.

"It's like time seems to stop up here. It's endless", Paige turns her head in my direction, and I drink her in. If only I could make time stop, slow down, trickle. Instead of it rushing towards us like a wave waiting to break the shore. If only.

We stand outside until Paige says she's cold and then we get back to the car and head home. Each time the turning to take her home comes towards us, Paige tells me to take a right instead of a left. And so we do that on and on and on, in a loop around her town, as though we can confuse time and hold onto this moment for as long as possible.

We drive and drive and drive. But even I know that it's not enough to outrace time.

Nothing ever will be.

Chapter Fifty

Paige

It feels like I've only just fallen asleep when my alarm goes off, an unwelcome shrill forcing me to open my eyes and get out of bed. Last night me and Lawrence drove and drove and drove and I wish I could capture that feeling in a bottle, that excitement and pleasure and contentment. If I could capture it in a bottle then I could at least remind myself on the hard days that there is still joy out there, that there are still things that make life worth it.

A glance at the clocks tells me I'm going to be late to meet Ari so I hurry and get dressed, ready for our walk in half an hour. Since it's cold outside, I throw on leggings and a sports bra and tie it together with a baggy sweatshirt to guard against the morning chill.

I send Lawrence a morning text as I head out the door, the hours spent talking to him felt so natural, I found myself opening up to him in ways I'd never opened up to anyone ever before. I told him about my sadness that slowly creeps up on me sometimes; the way my brain empties out for no reason at all and I feel so numb it almost feels like I don't exist. Even though telling him felt like the worse kind of treason to my fragile mind, it also felt like the first real step I've ever taken to making myself okay; to being okay with the sadness I couldn't explain. The ancients were right when they said a burden shared, is a burden halved.

Thoughts of Lawrence bring a smile to my lips as I walk to

the spot where I said I'd meet Ari. It's soon erased by anxiety when I spot Ari standing near a tree, waiting for me. I hope this won't be awkward, I've never turned someone down before, but I can't imagine it's a fun experience. Unless you're a sadist who delights in the torment and embarrassment of others. Which I'm definitely not.

"Hey", Ari beams when he sees me, leaning towards me as though for a kiss. I quickly turn my head to the side, so that his lips brush my cheek, instead of their intended destination: my lips. Ari's cheeks blush red in embarrassment, and I feel my own cheeks flush in turn, his embarrassment now becoming my own. I cough, trying to clear the awkward tension. Without even having started our walk, I know the lip-to-cheek kiss will haunt me into the early hours of the morning, playing on repeat in my mind when sleep eludes me.

"Hey", I finally say back, "shall we walk?".

"Sure", Ari sighs, no doubt already knowing where this conversation will end. We start with niceties, asking each other how our previous evenings were, both of us putting off the inevitable.

"Ari-", I say at the same time that he says.

"It's okay, don't worry". I let him speak. "I think I know what you're going to say, and it's okay. You don't like me as any more than friends, right?", he asks. I can't help but appreciate the directness.

"Yeah, I'm sorry. I have really enjoyed spending time with you, Brando, and Lillith. It was even nice doing something just the two of us, except just not in *that* way…", I blabber until a small smile appears across Ari's face.

"It's fine Paige, no hard feelings. You can't help your feelings; it is what it is". His adult approach to what I was dreading as an awkward conversation is refreshing. He genuinely doesn't seem all that bothered by it. I breathe a sigh of relief and offer Ari a genuine smile in return. We fall back into easy conversation, speaking about work. Ari tells me that Willis has broken up with his girlfriend, describing in vivid detail what went down as it happened whilst Ari was on shift with him. Apparently, Willis got into a rather heated debate with her on the phone whilst sitting in the staffroom, which I think is incredibly awkward, if not a little juicy.

The sun makes its appearance halfway into our walk, so that by the end, I'm all but a sweating mess, in need of a cold drink and a shower. We walk around the lake that takes up at least half the park, making sure to avoid all the angry swans and ugly, fluffy little goslings that follow their mom like soldiers following a general. I don't come here often but it really is a nice place. I can't help but think about how Lawrence would enjoy it; I can even picture him smiling down at the goslings in innocent wonder.

"This was nice, thanks Paige", Ari says as we slow down, coming back to where we started near the large, lumbering oak tree.

"It really was, and thank you for understanding", I say sheepishly.

"Don't be silly, there's nothing to understand". Ari smiles, but there's a twinge of sadness behind it.

"I'll see you at work next week then".

"Yeah you will", he winks at me and I take that as my queue to head home. I check my phone on the way back to my house and see that Lawrence had messaged me back saying morning whilst I was walking with Ari. I ask him what he's up to for the rest of the day, hoping that maybe I can see him if he's free. Since chatting to him last night on the phone, I've been overcome with this sense of peace, and although I can't quite put my finger on it, an intrinsic part of me knows it has to do with Lawrence.

I reach the driveway to my apartment before I feel my phone going off in my pocket.

"Hello", I answer without looking at who's calling.

"Hey Paige", Lawrence's voice comes through the speaker like a shockwave. "I thought we could do something in an hour or so, if you're free", he asks.

"Sure, want to meet me at mine in an hour and we can decide what to do then?", I ask. He agrees and is quick to get off the phone. I head into my apartment and fix some lunch before Lawrence comes, racking my brains for something we can do.

As I wash my plate up, I'm hit with an idea, hoping the sun stays out long enough that my plan isn't foiled by bad weather.

'Bring some swimming shorts and a towel'

I text Lawrence. Speech bubbles appear as he types his response. He sends a '?'. Wanting to be mysterious and leave the plans as a surprise, I text Lawrence back telling him to wait and see.

'See you soon'

he replies. I go and get ready and pack my bag whilst I wait for Lawrence to come.

Chapter Fifty-One

Lawrence

I meet Paige at hers with my things, curious to see what she has planned. Having never needed swimming shorts before, I've brought a pair of my training shorts with me instead. Paige leads us to her car which is parked just around the corner from her apartment.

"It isn't too long a drive from here", she grins, "half an hour tops". I smile back at her, her excitement infectious.

"Nice", I say. "Are you going to tell me where we're going?", I ask as she pulls out onto the road, the radio station white noise in the background.

"Not yet", she replies coyly. I turn my head towards the window and watch as the concrete turns to lush greenery, and I'm reminded of a time not so long ago when I took Paige to The Hills for a walk and the evening that ensued afterwards. Breaking the silence, I ask the question that has been on the tip of my tongue since the other day.

"So", I pause, too nervous to know the answer, "how was your date?". I slowly turn towards her, my whole being centred on whatever words next come out of her mouth.

"Oh", she stumbles, surprised by my question, "it was alright". *Alright?* Is she not going to elaborate?

"Only alright?", I probe, having to draw a further explanation out of her.

"I like Ari", if I had a heart, it seems to wilt at those words, "but only as a friend". And suddenly it's like the sun is shining on me again and I let out a sigh of relief. Not that I wouldn't want Paige to be happy if Ari did make her happy. There's just this little voice in the back of my head that whispers it should be me making her happy instead. I nod in her direction, unsure of what one says to something like that.

"If you look over there, you should be able to see our destination", Paige points her finger towards my side of the car. In the distance, I can see a river, the water glittering with rays of sunshine that are trying stubbornly to make it past the clouds. Paige pulls her car up along a quiet street and we both jump out.

"It's just a five-minute walk this way", Paige beckons, grabbing my hand and leading me towards the river. My hand feels clammy at the contact, and I can't stop looking at our joined hands as we walk across a small grassy field, made more navigable by a thin dirt track running through the centre.

"Ta da", Paige stops walking and gives a little flourish with her hands, turning in a small circle to take in the view. We're on the bank of a river, a little alcove secluded away from prying eyes by a large willow tree. The roots of the tree are big and expansive, snaking into the ground in a wide diameter and disappearing into the water. The long, flowing branches of the tree hang wistfully over the river's edge, a soft caress against the water, as though unable to resist the feel of the river against its branches. I take a step towards the edge and see that there are stone steps built into the side of the river closest to us, making entry into the water easier.

"It's safe to swim in. This spot was actually made for wild river swimming, hence the steps built into the bank", Paige explains as she slowly starts to undress. As her hands lift the bottom of her sweatshirt up, I feel an odd skipping sensation in my chest. I know the polite thing to do would be to turn away, but I find that my eyes are riveted to Paige in unending fascination. As a Reaper, I've seen countless naked bodies; the degree to which our charges are clothed as they die depends entirely on the circumstances of their deaths. So really, seeing Paige undress should be as uninteresting to me as the next dead body I see. And yet, I'm transfixed. She takes her jumper off first and then her leggings, leaving her baggy t-shirt until last. As each inch of skin is revealed, I feel a tightening sensation all over my body that I've never felt before. *Is this attraction?* Finally, she removes her t-shirt and reveals the plain, black bikini she's wearing underneath. She looks up at me and I'm not quick enough to avert my eyes. Instead, I step towards her, my hand coming to rest on her cheek. I kiss her slowly and delicately, my kiss giving voice to the attraction I feel. She steps away from me and gives me a shy smile.

"Are you coming?", she makes her way towards the edge of the bank, her feet asynchronously dipping into the water. I nod and start to undress; Paige is more chivalrous than I, using the time I get into my shorts to fully submerge herself in the water. A slight gasp is the only indicator of the chill. As I make my way to the edge of the bank, a nervous energy floods my system, both at the anticipation of the cold water, but also at the sight of Paige. Her wet hair now falls in rivulets down her back, her eyes made larger and bluer by having no hair framing them. Water sluices down her cheekbones and what I wouldn't do to wipe them away with the pad of my thumb. My first foot enters the water and it's all I can do to not immediately extricate it.

"I don't think I can do it", I choke out to Paige, and she laughs. The iciness of the water is so shocking, it takes my breath away, and I've only managed to go as far as my stomach. What takes my breath away more is the fact that, as a Reaper, the cold shouldn't really affect me. And yet here I am, my body trembling in the river, as if deprived of heat.

"It gets better once you go the whole way in", she grins devilishly and I'm not quite sure I believe her. Deciding to take a leap of faith, I dive towards Paige, plunging my head and shoulders into the murky blue river water. I stay under the water for a few seconds; the only sound is the hollow absence of it, a peaceful kind of emptiness that is unaffected by the chaos of the world above. Breaking the surface, I take a deep breath in, trying to compensate for the seconds where I was without oxygen. Again, a weird almost ominous feeling comes over me as I realise how much my body missed the ability to breathe for those few moments.

I'm drawn out of my unease as Paige moves towards me, swimming easily through the ripples as though she was born in the water. I follow after her, treading water clumsily, my body still acclimatising to the weightless feeling of being in the water. Once I get the hang of it, I let the water's current take me, enjoying the cold flush of water against my skin and the hush and hum of nature around me.

"Thank you", I turn towards Paige, overwhelmed with gratitude at being able to experience something so simple yet utterly indescribable.

"You're welcome. I love it here, it's so -", I cut her words off with my mouth, unable to resist touching her again. As I imagined, I let my thumb skim over the wayward water droplets that adorn her cheek and drink her into my body. She kisses me back with abandon, the naturalness of her against my skin feeling like nothing else. And then suddenly we've made our way back to the bank and I'm guiding Paige down onto her back. I hover above her and I swear, in all my centuries of existence, I've never seen something as captivating as her: her skin dewy from the river, the sun shines like polished dust on her cheeks making them rosy, her eyes so bright they're almost painful to look upon. She is so beautiful it feels like diving back into that cold water all over again: it takes my breath away.

Suddenly I'm moving on instinct, closing the distance between our bodies so that they are flush against one another. I rest my hand on Paige's hip so that I can feel her soft body against mine. I realise that this is it: I am on a precipice, a turning point in which there is no return. And all I want to do is leap off it and sink into Paige. My body moves on instinct, and I lose myself in Paige's flesh, the soft sounds I pull out of her and the primal sounds her body drags out of me.

And finally, I am alive.

This is living.

The fire in my veins is so exquisite that I fall.

And fall.

And fall.

Until I can no longer think around the pleasure in my blood. Suddenly I'm falling into the oblivion of the unknown, my limbs entwined with Paige's and her kisses the only lifeline I've ever needed. Once we're both spent, Paige's hand returns to my chest, her cheeks flushed with pleasure.

"Lawrence" she whispers, "your heart is racing". I lurch back, a queasy feeling overriding the pleasure. I sit back on my knees and place my hand on my chest, where Paige's just resided.

Da-dum. Da-dum. Da-dum.

A cold sweat of dread washes over me because she is right, my heart *is* racing.

My heart. My heart. My heart.

I have a heart, beating in my chest like a human's. In all my existence, I have never felt so at a loss for words as I do right now.

I look back at Paige and I see hurt crossing her features. Too wrapped up in the confusion of the last few days, I was careless in how my actions and body language might affect her. I lower myself back down to her side and kiss her forehead, luxuriating in the feel of her body, warm and solid against me.

"You make my heart race Paige and it's more than just a physical reaction". She peers up at me from where her head rests on my shoulder. "Being here with you gives me more meaning than I thought possible. You give me more than I deserve", I kiss her forehead again, indulging in such a simple yet intimate touch. *More than I'm allowed, is what I don't say.* And perhaps in those words, I've let slip more than I should, yet as she sighs against me, the compulsion to confess all my sins seems like the easiest thing in the world.

Instead, we lie in silence for hours and I find myself getting lost in Paige's body again and again and again.

This is it. This is what life was made for, this feeling right here.

***

We drive back to Paige's and I bid her farewell at her door, drawing her into my body for another kiss that is so decadent, I am at risk of an overdose. She closes the door behind her and I let myself sink into the Cosmos, heading straight to my room at Reaper HQ.

On my bed is the copy of *Looking for Alaska* that I had meant to return to Paige earlier. And it calls to me like a portent of my future: I can't help but feeling as though Paige is my very own Alaska, the appearance of her in my life the markable division between the existence I had before her and my life after.

Chapter Fifty-Two

Paige

With the Christmas holidays still ahead of me and uni work in the recesses of my mind, I'm lazy to get up this morning. After Lawrence said goodbye to me yesterday, I spent the rest of the night reliving the feeling of his hands on my body and the feel of him against me. It was one of those moments that will live with me always because it felt almost transcendent; it was more than just two bodies tangled together. In those moments, it felt like we were truly living – giving over to our desires and simply being in the present.

I'm working this evening but have the whole morning to myself. I managed to finish *Let It Snow* the other day at work, so now I get the excitement of picking something new to read. Knowing how small my to-be-read pile is, I decide to head into town to do some much-needed book shopping. I don't spend much time getting dressed as the weather is miserable and cold outside. Being a habitual recluse has taught me how to thrive in bad weather; my wardrobe is outfitted with the perfect items for such an occasion.

Dressed in my favourite outfit, a big, cream knitted jumper and flares, I throw on a coat to shield against the rain and head to my car. It takes about five minutes for my car to defog enough for me to drive safely and I faff about with what to play whilst it does. I play my most recently liked songs on Spotify, singing along to each and every song that comes on during my short car journey into town. I park about fifteen minutes away from the centre because car parking prices get more extortionate the closer to town you get. I'd rather spend any extra money on another book than fork out a tenner just to be able to park my car somewhere close. Despite the miserable weather, the walk is almost kind of enjoyable. The air outside smells fresh with the newness of rain and my mind seems to settle into the peacefulness of it. Even though I have my hood up, pesky drops of rain still manage to make their way underneath my hood, dampening the skin of my cheeks. Again, I'm reminded of Lawrence and everything we shared yesterday and I can't help but imagine everything else we could share if the pattern of our lives decides to take us in that direction.

I'm jostled about as I walk into the bookshop, many people seeming to be seeking shelter from the rain, sitting on one of the perches right next to the shop window, rather than having actual interest in the treasures beyond. I head to level two to find the fantasy section, already eager to run my hands over the unmarred spines of new books and survey what the bookshop has on offer for me today. The walk up the two flights of stairs, in my many layers and waterproof coat that now seems to be a heat insulter, is almost agony, but I would walk for miles for the taste of unventured stories and slow-burn enemies-to-lovers plot lines. As I make my way to the shelves of books, I mentally take note of all the books I've already read, an internal monologue of those I liked and those I couldn't even finish resounding in my head.

"That book is one of my favourites", I blurt out to a girl turning over one of the fantasy books I've read time and again, the plot full of fae males, love triangles, and intrigue. "Sorry", I laugh "but if there's one book you should leave with today, *A Court of Thrones and Roses* is definitely one of them". And I can't help but be proud of myself for even speaking to this stranger; Paige from a few weeks ago would have wanted to recommend the book but would have been too shy to say anything.

"I've heard good things about it. But I wasn't sure if it's just overhyped", she laughs, tucking the book into her elbow, evidence of her taking my recommendation on board.

"I think it's slightly overhyped, but the hype is definitely worth it", I exclaim.

"I'll definitely buy it then!", she excitedly replies.

"Maybe we could exchange numbers and meet up for a coffee or something to discuss it once you've finished it. I'm always looking for people to share my passion for books with", feeling slightly awkward but knowing that putting myself out of my comfort zone is good for me.

"That would be so fun", her enthusiasm makes me glad I asked. She gives me her phone and I enter my contact details, wishing her a good time reading. Thanking me, she tells me her name is Elyza and promises to message me when she's ready to discuss it. I wave goodbye and make my way over to the bookshelves, each colourful spine one more addition waiting to happen. I spend at least twenty minutes going back and forth on which books to buy; those that I don't purchase today, I've added to an ever-growing list I keep on a notes page on my phone. I take my five brand new books to the counter, wishing I didn't have to work later so I could start devouring one of them instead.

Books in hand, I grab a coffee for the drive home and take a slow walk back to my car. I place my books on the passenger seat, veritable companions I'm ready to get to know. When I get home, I organise my books on my shelf and head upstairs to get ready for work. As I'm getting dressed, I see my phone ping with a message from Elyza: it's a picture of the book and a coffee, telling me she's starting it now. I react to the image with a heart and tell her I can't wait to discuss it. It feels exciting to have made another potential friend to share my passion for reading with. I'm proud of myself for making that connection and smile to myself as I potter about. I decide to text Lawrence and ask if wants to go for food after my shift has finished, deciding to keep grabbing life by the horns. He replies straight away, saying he'd love to. My heart does a little dance at his reply and I take a moment to bask in this happiness. I made a new friend today and now there's this possibility for something *more* with Lawrence. And of course, it isn't love; love isn't something that just falls in your lap the second you meet someone. But that kindling flame of *something* I felt the first time I locked eyes with him at the cemetery could be nurtured into a fire so scorching it takes my breath away. It isn't love, yet. But someday it could be. I think I could fall for someone like him, if given the chance. Although this is just one day and microscopic in the grand scheme of my whole life, this contentedness feels like a turning point for me; it seems like I have something more than just books and fictional characters to live for.

Chapter Fifty-Three

Lawrence

I'm distracted. And have been all day. My mind is still with Paige on that river, even if my physical body is here in HQ, going over drills and drills and drills in training, until all I hear is the thumping of my heart in my chest. The training hall is empty and thank fuck for that. My heart thuds so loud in my ears, I'd be surprised if Anchor can't hear it from his office. That tingle I've come to know so well starts at the nape of my neck, but I ignore it, at least for a little while. I cannot quite describe this hesitation, but after yesterday, after being given that small glimpse of life, I cannot find it in me to hasten anyone's end.

I slowly make my way to the showers, where I can wash off the sweat from training and hopefully let the water soothe away all the things I've slowly opened myself up to. My mind wrapped up in the taste of Paige on my lips and the ache I feel in my chest at thoughts of her being gone, I don't notice Elodie until her hand is on my forearm and she's turning me around to face her.

"Law", she says, and her tight inhalation seems to speak a thousand words neither one of us will risk inside the walls of HQ. "I called your name twice, didn't you hear me?". She steps back, looking me up and down.

"No, sorry", I say, making to move away from her. I don't have the energy to listen to her question me, her eyes saying all the things she's unwilling to verbalise.

"I need to talk to you", she presses, "it's important Law".

"Can it wait, my next charge is ready. I was just heading there now", even if I was going to shower to put off reaping for a short while, it's not entirely a lie.

"No, Law, it can't. I -"

"Later, El, I promise", I say and carry on walking to the showers. She mutters something under her breath, but I can't quite make out what it is; the great hearing that I've known for so long suddenly a muffled echo of what it's always been.

In the showers, I strip down and turn the water as cold as my body can now handle, which is barely a degree below lukewarm. The cold shower brings forth the iciness of the river water and I'm drowning in feeling. The physical feeling of Paige's skin against my own, deepened by this inexpressible warmth in my chest when I think of her. When her face appears in my mind, it feels like I'm falling; getting lost in thoughts of her until I don't know where I begin and these feelings for her end. I can see why all the great poets elevate romance to the highest echelon of human feeling; there's a completeness to it that one doesn't even realise they need until they find themselves whole through the affection of another.

In the back of my mind, I let my Reaper senses drift to Paige and watch voyeuristically as she picks up one book then five, her excitement at all the books flooding me, until I too feel her passion for reading resonate through me. Not wanting to spy on her any longer, I turn the shower off and dry myself. I take note of the harsh texture of the towel on my skin, abrasive and rough, like it's trying to strip me down layer by layer. I throw the towel in the communal wash basket and grab some of the spare clothes I keep in the locker room. Dressed, and with no other reason to linger, I drift away to my next charge.

***

I arrive at what seems to be an amusement park, that tether inside me guiding me towards a ramshackle building with a big sign saying 'Fun House', hanging crookedly over the front door.

I go inside and am surrounded by mirrors upon mirrors upon mirrors. I walk through the maze of mirrors, startled every so often by a distorted image of myself. In one mirror I am short and wide, in another, so tall and skeletal it's like seeing myself in my true form. That knot in my chest tells me to keep walking, down hall after hall of mirrors until I finally see the door at the end of the hallway. I walk through the door at the end of the hall and find myself back outside. There's a small sea of people milling about on the grass eating food from stalls, children screaming at the clowns that walk past them. Confused, I go to step back inside the fun house, but the door is locked from the inside. That tingle at the back of my neck intensifies as I step towards the door again, trying the handle one last time. I step away and the sensation fades with it.

My Reaper sense is telling me that the next person on my list is in that room, but the only person in there was me. I didn't see another living soul the entire time I walked through those halls of mirrors. I frown, Anchor's words about the slight mayhem of the Universe the only explanation I can think of for such a thing. I leave the fun house, walking towards the stalls of food, letting the smell of fresh popcorn and candyfloss wash over me. My phone buzzes in my pocket as I buy some candy floss, the airy texture dissolving on my tongue with a sickly sweetness. It's Paige, asking to see me later. I don't even have to think before my finger pens a reply, telling her I'd meet her after work.

The puzzle of the charge I couldn't find is replaced by the soft anticipation of seeing Paige later; I'm too hung up on the possibilities of what could be, to let confusion and apprehension ruin my happy feelings. I wander aimlessly around the amusement park, taking it all in, killing time until Paige's shift is over. I see couples laugh and smile. An old man and woman sit quietly on a bench, watching what I can only assume to be their grandchildren run wildly in circles, chasing one another. Their hands are clasped together in their laps, their faces mapped with the lines their lives have left behind on their skin. A pang of regret and jealousy runs through me at the precious gift that the Universe granted them: to spend a lifetime with each other. A part of me imagines that that could be Paige and I in fifty years, if the Universe wasn't so cruel and unexpected. I linger watching them, living a life well lived vicariously through them, knowing the time I have with Paige is slowly coming to an end.

Sadness washes over me as I make my way towards Paige, the image of the old, happy couple behind my eyelids, the picture of a dream I never knew I wanted, but now crave like a madman craves sanity.

Chapter Fifty-Four

Paige

My shift at work passes with little excitement. It was pretty quiet tonight, so I managed to get the cleaning done in less time than it normally takes. Using the last half an hour of my shift to get ready for Lawrence, I grab my bag from my locker and sneak off to the changing rooms for a quick shower and change. I put on flared jeans, ripped at the knees, a Harley Davidson top and my leather jacket, the smell of chlorine clinging to my skin, despite scrubbing furiously at it in the shower for five minutes straight. Thoughts of Lawrence pull me into reception, the anticipation of seeing him enough to make my heart stop, and then race twice as fast in the span of thirty seconds. My manager tells me if everything is done that I can head off, so I leave ten minutes earlier than anticipated. To my surprise, Lawrence is already here. I texted him the address earlier, saying to meet me here as I know a nice place around the corner.

"Hey", I call as I walk towards him and he pulls me in for a hello kiss, his hand resting on my waist as he pulls me in close. I feel my face flush at the open display of affection, something I've never really been used to.

"Hey", he smiles against my lips, stepping back and looking me over. "You look beautiful Paige, as always". Although his hand is no longer around my waist, it's drifted to my own hand, now casually holding it between his.

"I thought I could leave my car here and we can walk to the

restaurant. It's about a fifteen-minute walk", I say as I put my things in my car and lock it again, all one handed, since Lawrence's hand still holds the other.

"Sure", Lawrence says and tells me to lead the way. So I do.

The night sky has darkened, the dark sky mottled with wisps of grey from persistent clouds that threaten another downpour. The quiet streets slowly start to fill with people the closer we get to the precinct where the Mexican bar is.

"How was your day, did you get up to anything interesting before work?", Lawrence asks with the beginnings of a smile on the corner of his lips.

"Yeah, I went shopping for new books actually. I think I may have even made a new friend", I beam, again proud of myself for something so small to most but a big deal for me. Lawrence smiles down at me, my excitement washing over him. He leans in and presses a kiss to my temple.

"Paige, that's", he pauses, "I'm proud of you", he whispers. Just hearing those words makes my eyes water because it's like he can see all the way through me; he can see how desperately hard interacting with new people is for me and yet I've done it anyway. And Lawrence is the reason for that. In his own way, he's been the catalyst for my new fervour for life.

I change the subject quickly before I embarrass myself by bursting into tears. I ask him how his day was. He pauses before answering, as if unsure of what to share. "It was... strange", he settles on, a furrow appearing on his brow showing his confusion. He doesn't elaborate and I'm polite enough to let it go, enjoying just being in his company too much to pry into things he clearly doesn't wish to discuss. The slow trickle of Mexican music interrupts the quiet lull we've fallen into since Lawrence's last words.

"It's just around the corner now", I say into the quiet.

The restaurant is on the corner of the next road, its lime green door and colourful lanterns making it glow against the dark of the evening sky. The front wall of the restaurant is glass that opens on warm nights to let guests sit out under the stars. On the brick wall next to the restaurant is a street painting of a skeleton, fashioned after the Day of the Dead festival. Lawrence runs his hand over the hollow eyes and bright florals of the painting, lingering for a moment before coming to my side on the front step.

"They make skeletons seem almost beautiful", he whispers, more to himself than me, as the waiter approaches.

"Table for two please", Lawrence says and we're ushered inside. We're led to a cosy booth table at the back of the restaurant; a deep velvet sofa framed by chunky glass lanterns and caricatures of macho wrestlers hung haphazardly on the wall.

"After you", I scoot into the corner of the booth and Lawrence follows, sitting at the bend of the table so we're not quite next to, yet not quite opposite, each other either.

"Here are your menus, I'll be back shortly to take your order", the waiter says before heading back to the front door to seat a family of five. Ever the creature of habit, I'll be ordering what I have every time I've come here, but that doesn't stop me from looking at the menu anyway. Everything is written in Spanish with English translations underneath, with sombrero hats separating each course.

"Do you know what you'll get?", Lawrence asks, his fingers absently tracing the outline of the menu.

"Yeah, the tacos here are really good so I normally order those".

"Maybe I'll try them too", he smiles. The waiter comes back over and we order two portions of chicken tacos with chips and a jug of table water. The waiter comes back with the water for the table and then me and Lawrence are left in relative solitude. Lawrence picks up the jug and pours us each a glass. The soft lap of water against my glass reminds me of the rushing river yesterday. I peek a glance at Lawrence, heat making my cheeks red, as he puts the jug back on the table.

"Yesterday was something else Paige", Lawrence blurts out, almost as if the water too reminded him of the river. "It will live inside of me always". The way he says that last line makes my heart trip over itself. Like it's goodbye.

"Lawrence", I begin, but he cuts me off.

"Please don't say anything else Paige. Please", he begs, a sorrow so potent behind his words, it's like a punch through my chest. Not understanding why but also not wanting to make his unknown pain worse, I nod hesitantly. "So", I say, trying to dispel some of the tension, "do you have much planned for the Christmas holidays?".

"No concrete plans yet", his eyes light up as though he's just thought of something, "but maybe if you're around we could spend some of it together?".

"Yeah, I'd love that", I smile at him. "I'll probably go visit my family for a few days but you could help me put my Christmas tree up if you'd like?". It would be nice to have someone to do that with, to share that experience with.

"Really?", such excitement radiates off him that it's infectious. I nod enthusiastically, made speechless by the sheer beauty of him. On any given day he's handsome, but with that smile lighting up his eyes, he's breathtaking. Just at that moment, the waiter comes back to the table with our food, saving me from blurting out just how mesmerising I think he is.

The smell alone makes my stomach rumble, so I dig in without waiting another second. Taking a minute to drag myself away from the perfect blend of salt and sour, I ask Lawrence what he thinks of the food.

"It's really good", he says as he finishes his last taco, having wolfed them down at double the speed I've eaten mine, "so good", he grins.

"All done?", the waiter asks once we've finished eating. We both nod along.

"Yes, it was really good, thank you", Lawrence replies.

"Is there anything else I can get for you?".

"Just the bill please", I say. As we wait for the waiter to bring the bill over, Lawrence picks my hand up off the table, threading his fingers through with mine.

"Here you go", the waiter places the bill on the table, and Lawrence has scooped it up before I've even had time to blink. He hands the waiter the cash, grinning at me devilishly.

"It was my turn to pay", I protest.

"I like treating you Paige, so please let me", Lawrence says as he places kisses where our hands are joined. "Ready to go?".

"Yes", I nod, trying but failingly miserably to scoot out of the booth gracefully. I just about make it to my feet without falling over, but only just.

Lawrence leads me out of the restaurant and back the way we came, running his hand over the skeleton painting on the wall outside the restaurant. Across the street is a neon sign that says karaoke, people spilling out the front door as though there's not enough space inside. Lawrence's head kicks to the side as though intrigued and he's pulling me across the street without second thought.

"Shall we?", he asks, tilting his head to the neon orange sign, the blare of a microphone hitting our ears now we're close enough to the entrance.

"It's not really my scene, if I'm honest", I shake my head, "but I guess there's no harm in going in", I say as his shoulders seem to deflate with disappointment. I take his hand and lead him inside, his excitement washing over me. There's a set of stairs that lead down into the bar, the cheap vinyl floor sticky with remnants of dropped alcohol.

215

"Who would like to go next?", a towering man with a beard shouts into the microphone.

"We will", Lawrence pulls me towards the elevated wooden platform, meant to be a stage, at the front of the room, his hand in the air to get the burly man's attention.

"Lawrence, no", I shout over the din in the bar, dragging in my heels in an attempt to slow him down.

"Come on up then", waving his hand towards the microphone stand, the burly-man moves off the stage.

"Please Paige", Lawrence whispers to me as he positions me in front of the microphone, his lips pouted, eyes like puppies in his bid to get me to agree.

"Fine", I roll my eyes, my stomach doing somersaults as he drags his teeth over his bottom lip, "but only one song". The music starts just as I finish speaking and the familiar intro of *Grease* blares through the speakers. I give Lawrence a quizzical look, as if to ask how he knows this song, it certainly doesn't seem like the type of music he'd casually listen to.

"This is a classic Paige, anyone alive for the last fifty years would know it", he winks and begins singing Danny's opening lines. And despite what he's just said, I'm surprised he even knows the words. Although his permanent wardrobe of black t-shirts and trousers fits the Danny Zuko vibe, he never struck me as the type to listen to musicals, let alone know the words. Lawrence turns his head in my direction as Sandy's lines come onto the mini television screen in front of us. Clearing my throat, I nervously sing into the microphone. Lawrence moves towards me and grabs my hand, twirling me around the stage. The smile on his face is so big it's infectious and I forget that we're in a room full of people and let Lawrence's joy rub off on me as we sing and dance along to the music. He sings that I'm the one that he wants and butterflies take flight in my stomach at how happy those words make me. And even though it's just a song, the bright glint in his eyes tells me those words ring true. The song ends and Lawrence pulls me towards him, energy pouring off him in waves.

"Thank you", he says, smiling against my lips as he pulls me in for a kiss.

"That was kind of fun", I smile, kissing him back, "so thank you", I place a playful kiss on his cheek and drag him off the stage, lest we get heckled for too much PDA. Lawrence threads his arm around my waist, and I soak in the warmth of his skin on mine. Even though it's just the beginning, I feel like I'm falling for the potential of us, the smile I'm unable to wipe off my face living proof of my happiness.

Chapter Fifty-Five

Lawrence

We walk out of the bar, and I can't help but look forward to the future. Maybe if I deny the job I need to do, it will go away. Maybe I can spend the holidays with Paige first, experience Christmas and all it entails, before I'm doomed to take her life away.

On the walk back to Paige's car, we pass by a large house already decked-out in Christmas paraphernalia and I'm hit with such longing and excitement to do something as mundane as decorating a Christmas tree. I can already see it in my mind: Paige in a big woolly jumper and tinsel stuck in her hair, smiling freely and unashamedly as I pull the top of the tree down to place the star on top. Once the tree is decorated, we'll sit on her sofa, breathing in the smell of pine needles whilst a Christmas film plays on the tv and I lose myself in her for hours on end.

"What are you smiling at?" Paige asks.

"You", I tell her. Instead of replying, she stops me in the middle of the street, people giving us dirty looks as they try and navigate around us, and kisses me with uncontrolled abandon.

Paige kisses me and, the Universe be damned, I kiss her back as if my very world depends on it. I pull her close to me and in this moment, nothing has ever seemed to matter as much as how she feels against me. As I kiss her, my mind conjures up moments from the last few weeks: my first taste of Chinese food, the melodic sound of Paige laughing, the intricacies of the human anatomy, immersing myself in a fictional world until the pages in front of me became all I know; Paige's skin against mine, a tangle of limbs and breaths and desire so potent it hurts. The ache of living a newfound sensation I didn't know I wanted until I found Paige.

The thing is, the last few weeks I've begun to understand how precious time is and how important it is to let the people who mean something to you know that. And Paige hasn't come to mean just something, she means *everything*. I am in awe of her. And even though we still have some time left, in this moment, nothing is more urgent to me than letting her know how I feel. A light tingle prickles the back of my neck, like the Universe is agreeing with me for once.

I close my eyes and breathe.

Noisy people and the blare of cars come rushing back as I open my eyes and the world around me comes back into focus. Concern lines Paige's features as my eyes settle on her before me.

"Paige", I say, a sigh leaving my body as tell myself to tell her how much she's come to mean to me, whilst I still can. She opens her mouth, to say what, I don't know. I don't let her speak, instead I kiss her, revelling in the feel of her on my lips. I pull her out of the way of moving people, onto a quiet alley.

I kiss her and close my eyes, this kiss a culmination of the ones that came before.

I pull back slightly, just enough to see her face, to lose myself in her eyes, an ocean so deep I could drown in them.

"Paige, I'm sorry", I kiss her lips as though pressing my apology into her skin.

"Sorry?", she asks, confusion furrowing her brow, a small worry line etched into her forehead.

"I'm sorry for not showing up for our presentation and I'm sorry for wasting the weeks we could have spent together. But I was being stubborn, I –", I stop talking, a lump in my throat so painful I can't force words past it. How do I put into words what she makes me feel when it's all so new to me? I run my thumb along her cheekbone, etching the feel of her skin beneath mine into my soul.

"Lawrence", she smiles, hope and longing filling her gaze, "we've got time, a few missed weeks is nothing in the grand scheme of things", she laughs. Standing on her tiptoes, she presses a kiss to my lips. And it isn't soft or tame, it's hungry, the taste of my lips inciting a passionate war in her, she threads her hands in my hair, and I'm lost in the feel of being *wanted* by her. I push her against the brick wall, one hand in her tousled hair, the other framing her head against the wall. She pulls on my shirt, dragging me closer to her, and we stay like that for minutes or seconds, I cannot say.

It's both infinite and transitory.

"You have made me feel things I never thought possible", I pull away, my fingers tracing the path my lips have just trailed on her lips. I touch her eyes, her cheeks, the soft skin of her neck, every inch of her a map I want to travel. I place my palm above her heart, feeling it beat erratically for me. "It's funny", I muse, more to myself than Paige, "I always thought humans dramatic in their search for something as insubstantial as love. It isn't something you can see, so how could it possibly be something worthy of losing yourself over?".

"But I find I'm losing myself in you Paige. I see you around every corner I walk, chasing just another moment I can hold onto you. Before you I was nothing. *Nothing*. And now I'm made in your image. You have breathed life into me. You've filled me with *longings* and a happy ending I never knew could taste so bittersweet as it does right now. You are everything I never wanted but now find myself broken knowing that I will have to live on without you. I may continue to exist, but I will die when your soul dies; your face will haunt me until I dissolve into nothing. And even then, not enough time will have passed to erase these emotions that swim inside me at just the thought of you. I was nothing before you and, without you, I will become nothing again. I have spent centuries as a husk of a man, not knowing I was waiting for something, *someone*, to make me want to live. And I would go through many centuries more for just a few more seconds spent with you. Because this time together Paige", I brush my lips along hers, breathing her into my memories, "it has been *everything*. You are everything". I finally stop talking, the need to confess to her ebbing away with each word.

"You're not making sense Lawrence", Paige shakes her head, a sad smile taking over her features.

"Please just know that it has been my entire purpose to know you Paige". I place both hands on the wall behind her head and slowly lower my lips to hers, trapping her here. Holding onto this moment for as long as I can, as I know we only have numbered moments like this left. She shakes her head, but says nothing else, comfortable in the cage of my arms and the hunger of my kisses.

"Everything", I whisper, planting one last kiss on Paige's forehead before I pull my arms back to my sides. I finally pull myself out of the reverie I've been in, ready to continue the rest of the night. I step away from Paige.

I hear her call my name, but I'm too caught up in my rushing thoughts and feelings that I can't hear what she's saying. Finally admitting what I've not let myself think: that I know I won't be able to do the job I must. But as I begin to cross the busy road, it occurs to me that the bond that has connected me to Paige since the first moment my eyes met hers in the cemetery has changed, transformed into something new. It no longer feels like the tingle of Death.

I begin to cross the busy road, suddenly hopeful. Maybe the Universe has granted me a boon – maybe in my indulgence of getting to know Paige, the Universe decided that maybe she did deserve a chance at life after all. I don't know what that means for me, but that small relief is all I can think of as I make my way across the busy road. Too caught up in my relief for Paige, I don't see the flash of headlights on the road as I step out. Too concerned with looking at Paige, whose face is now contorted in horror as she reaches towards me, I don't quite realise what is happening until it's already too late. A noiseless scream leaves her lips as light swallows me whole and pain like I could never have imagined floods my body.

Epilogue

Elodie

Love and death are in many ways the same: inexpressible, overwhelming, constant, and forever. But where love brings you alive, Death wraps his hollow arms around you, making you painfully aware of the arms that will never hold you again, the physical touch of humanity that is no longer open to you.
How do you tell someone they're gone? How do you make known to them something unknowable? It's not something you can quite verbalise, but is instead a feeling, that touch of our hands as we beckon the passing souls into their afterlife.
I watch as Paige stands alone on the street, her hand at her throat as silent tears mark rivers of agony down her cheeks. Law's body lies lifeless on the road, his spirit reaching towards Paige as though she is the only lighthouse he will ever need to guide him home. The flashing lights of the ambulance paint Paige's pale skin blue, her hand moving from her throat to her chest, where the ghost of Law's hands rest, as though his feelings for her transcends all earthy plains.
"Law", I whisper, and he turns his head reluctantly towards me, denial radiating off him in waves. Holding my hand out towards him, I let him look at Paige one last time before the world falls away.
"El?", he looks at me, horror dawning on his face as he realises where we are. "What", he chokes out and he can't even finish his sentence. I feel tears slide down my face as he shakes his head.

And even though Anchor told me to remain professional, how can I? It's Law.

"It was never about Paige, Law", I start, the words that will bring him enlightenment flowing from me as freely as the tears down my face. "You could feel it, couldn't you? That Paige was different, and I didn't believe you, not until we were in your room and I saw your name appear on my list. That's when I knew it was about you. Paige being your charge wasn't a way for you to help her become accustomed with Death. In helping her live, she granted you that which is always denied to Reapers: life".

"I don't understand". Law says, his soul blinking in and out of existence as he grapples with his reality.

"That's the thing about life. It's not there to be understood. It just is. Although you didn't have the chance to fall in love with Paige, or her with you, she gave you the chance to fall in love with the potential of love, of what it means to be alive, of humanity. I can't answer why it's happened to you Law. Life is a riddle that no one person will ever have the answer to. All humans can do is be present in their own life and trust that it all adds up to some bigger something. That is what it means to be alive. To trust that every action adds up to something more and, when it's over, be it after twenty years or eighty, knowing that you made the most of what you were granted whilst you could". Law shudders, the reality of my words washing over him like a balm. Law opens his mouth and closes it again, words seeming to fail him.

Law doesn't answer me straight away, instead looking past me to where Paige stands, tears still falling down her cheeks. He lifts his hand as though reaching for her, whispering three words over and over again: "you were everything". And although Paige can no longer hear him, her head turns slightly as if his words echo somewhere within her.

"I never knew life could be like that El", Law says, finally turning back to me. "I didn't realise how vital being connected to someone else is. It isn't just that humans romanticise loving someone else, it's so much more than just a fantasy: they find who they are through the affections of someone else". He pauses, tears falling down his cheeks, liquid heralds of his end. "I found who I was through Paige, she - she made me El", he chokes, bringing a shaking hand to his lips "she gave me everything".

We stand in silence then, filled with words neither of us know how to say. The absence of speech seems to say it all.

"It's time Law", I move towards him, my hand outstretched towards his own. Blinking away his final tears, Law takes my hand and we fade away to The Beyond. We stand watching souls float past, charting the path Law is soon to make.

"Paige", he says, his final words echoing around the void of the Cosmos. "Paige". He lets go of my hand and follows the sea of bright lights ahead.

"Goodbye Law", I say, wiping the last wayward tears from my eyes. His soul floats towards The Beyond, a white light fading into the distance.

Goodbye Lawrence.

Acknowledgements

As someone who's dream it's been to always publish a book, writing the acknowledgement section feels so surreal! I've really done it. Thus with a Kiss has been a 2 year journey and seeing how Paige and Lawrence's story evolved is a journey that I'll always hold close to my heart, both because it's the first novel I've actually finished in full, after years of half-arsed attempts and unfinished stories. But also because I wrote this book during a time where sometimes what I wanted out of life seemed so far out of reach. And even though some days I'm still navigating life like a sailor lost at sea, perhaps a bit lost and unsure and hopeless, seeing the physical copy of my debut novel brought to life will always now be the lighthouse of hope to guide me through life during moments of uncertainty. This book means so much to me for many different reasons and I'm so grateful to finally be sharing it with the world.

Firstly, I'd like thank my twin sister Lyd, who's always encouraged me with my writing and who I can always count on to big me up and be my biggest fan. I also wouldn't have had the gusto to make my bookstagram account, if not for you cheering me on from post one! Paige & Lawrence's story wouldn't be what it was if not for our multiple brainstorming sessions and your meticulous attention to detail. As well as your newfound career as a graphic designer.

I'd also like to thank my mom, dad, and Meg who, like Lyd, have always supported me. Growing up in our family has taught me how special it is to be so close and I'm grateful for all the moments over the years where I've been able to lean on you.

Next on my list is my book club – Lyd (again!) and Matthew. Thank you for being the first readers of my book! It was an honour to share it with you. It seems surreal that you'll now have the physical copy, when before I sent you a mere word document!

I'd also like to give Eva a shoutout, who encouraged me to start my blog and website, as well as my bookstagram page. And though she may not be a reader, she did her best to read the first half on my book when I gave it to her! Our friendship means so much to me and I hope you finally get round to reading the rest of the book!

I'd also like to thank Tom (and Lyd) for letting me use your house as a writing studio during my garden leave and giving me the space to focus and finally finish my first draft!

Tom Garrat, a screenwriter and unlikely writing friend – thank you for taking the time to read Paige & Lawrence's story, and the hundreds of updates I got along the way! Even if we didn't quite agree on the ending, I truly appreciate all the feedback you gave.

I'd also like to thank my bookstagram and booktok community for supporting me. I wish I'd made my accounts sooner because I've truly met some lovely people along the way who allow me to share my passion for reading with and have helped me come out of my shell.

Lastly, I'd like to thank you, reader. Thank you for supporting me and reading Paige and Lawrence's story until the end. It means more than you know that you went on this journey with me. And even though Paige and Lawrence's story wasn't graced with a happy ending, if there's one thing I wish you to take away, long after the last page has been read, is that life is precious. Life is short and inconstant; it is sad and happy, invigorating and hopeless. But it is yours. Yours to claim, yours to cherish, yours to do with in any way that brings you joy. So please, dear reader, make your life count. Because it's the only one you'll get.

Social Media Links

Keep up-to-date with all my latest writing and follow me on socials!

Instagram: @words_byamie
TikTok: @words_byamie
Website: www.wordsbyamie.wordpress.com/

If you enjoyed reading it, please don't forget to leave it a review on Goodreads and Amazon as well as telling all your friends and family! :)

Printed in Great Britain
by Amazon